"You're turning your back on the world!"

Blaise's voice was grim and accusing. "You're saying safety is more important than risk—that you're afraid to take a chance!"

"But I'm blind!" Shannon cried defensively. "And I don't like being laughed at! When I go out I stumble. I spill things—"

"Do you want to spend the rest of your days closeted at home with your mother?" he interrupted brutally. "You're young, you're beautiful and you could be very much alive...."

Blaise grasped her shoulders as he spoke. The tension snapped between them; he dragged her into his arms. Shannon felt a flash of fire as his lips descended on hers.

When he finally spoke again his voice was husky. "The choice is yours, Shannon."

Sight of a Stranger

by

SANDRA FIELD

Harlequin Books

TORONTO • LONDON • LOS ANGELES • AMSTERDAM
SYDNEY • HAMBURG • PARIS • STOCKHOLM • ATHENS • TOKYO

Original hardcover edition published in 1981
by Mills & Boon Limited

ISBN 0-373-02480-0

Harlequin edition published June 1982

CHAPTER ONE

THE day he arrived was a day like any other; Shannon had no premonition of change, no intuitive sense that her life was never to be the same again.

It had rained most of the day, the soft, persistent Pacific coast drizzle that had given the grass its brilliant green hue. She knew that water droplets must be clinging to the drooping heads of the daffodils and collecting in the scarlet goblets of the Darwin tulips. Once, as a little girl, Shannon had tried to drink from one of the tulips and had discovered a drowned ant in the bottom; now, as she sat quietly by the French doors that led to the garden, she remembered this, and a faint reminiscent smile curved her lips. She had spat the water out, she recalled, and her mother, horrified, had reproved her bad manners. It all seemed a very long time ago. . . .

She shifted in her chair. She spent too much time dwelling on the past nowadays—but what else was there to do? Closing her eyes, her fingers digging into the delicate gilded arms of the antique chair, Shannon fought back the suffocating despair that always seemed to be hovering around her, waiting for the slightest moment of weakness to pounce and envelop her.

It was then that she heard the sound of a car coming to a halt in front of the house. Her hearing had sharpened preternaturally in the last few months, and she knew immediately from the well-bred purr of its motor that it was an expensive car. A door slammed. Footsteps crossed the gravel and ran briskly up the front steps— masculine footsteps, she was sure. Those of a man very confident and sure of himself. Certainly it was not Dr

Snider, their family doctor, or Colonel Fawcett, her mother's bridge partner. The doorbell pealed, and to her over-sensitive imagination it seemed as though even that had a touch of impatience, of command. She heard Bridget push open the swing door from the back hall and cross the thick carpeting to the door, then the click of the latch as she opened it.

'Good evening.' A deep masculine voice, whose timbre made the girl in the chair shudder with recognition. 'Could you tell me if Miss Hart is home, please?'

'Why, yes, she is, sir. Come this way, please.'

The voice echoed in Shannon's brain. It was Rick—after all these months he had come back to her . . . back where he belonged. Ridiculously, all she could think of was that she had not washed her hair and that the dress she was wearing was an old one her mother had chosen for her and that she herself had never liked.

'You're sitting in the dark again, child,' Bridget chided with the ease of long familiarity. She pulled the switch and from the wall brackets a muted light fell on the room. In one swift glance the visitor encompassed it. Massive Victorian furniture encroached on the faced Persian rug, while from the gold-flocked wallpaper dark-visaged ancestors stared at him in disapproval. The tall windows were shrouded by elaborately pleated drapes, whose heavy folds would permit only the minimum of daylight to penetrate on the sunniest of days. The room was obsessively tidy, with no signs of daily occupancy or use, and it was this that brought the man's gaze to the girl in the chair.

She had half risen and was staring at him with a kind of strained intensity. Before he could speak, she whispered, 'Rick, is it really you? You don't know how I've longed for you to come back!' Her hands were clasped at her breast in unconscious appeal as her smile broke through, irradiating her face with joy. 'Come closer——'

The visitor took a half step towards her, then halted in frustration, his fists clenched at his sides. 'I'm sorry,' he said roughly. 'I'm not Rick. My name is Blaise Strathern—I'm Rick's half-brother.'

The girl looked as though he had struck her. The radiance vanished from her face, leaving it pinched and pale as she shrank back into the chair. The catch in her throat sounded shockingly loud in the ornately furnished room. 'You're not Rick?' she faltered. 'You're his half-brother? I didn't even know he had one.'

'It's not surprising he wouldn't mention me to you,' was the grim reply. 'To put it mildly, we've never got along particularly well together.'

'Your voice is very much like his.' There was a tinge of doubt, a questioning, in her statement.

'I'm not Rick.'

Belatedly Shannon tried to pull herself together. 'What name did you say?'

'Blaise. Pronounced "blaze" but spelled B-l-a-i-s-e.'

'A French name?'

'Yes. My mother was French.'

Something in his voice forbade further questions. Helplessly Shannon said, 'Bridget, perhaps Mr Strathern would like a drink?'

'A Scotch and soda, please.'

'Certainly, sir. Shannon, what could I get you, dearie?'

'A sherry would be fine, Bridget.'

The older woman left the room and a constrained silence fell over its two remaining occupants. Shannon's head was whirling with questions, none of which she had the courage to ask, while Blaise Strathern seemed content to sit in silence. Looking in his direction, she finally said with careful politeness, 'Do you live on the west coast, Mr Strathern?'

'No, at the moment I'm based in Quebec.'

Another silence. Shannon bit her lip, then thankfully

her head swung towards the door as she heard the rustle of Bridget's starched uniform.

'Here's your drink, sir,' the maid said comfortably. 'I'll put yours on the table beside your chair, Shannon.'

'Thank you, Bridget.' Carefully her hand curved around the fragile crystal as she raised the glass to her lips. 'To a pleasant stay in the west, Mr Strathern.'

She heard the ice clink in his glass as he put it down. 'Look,' he said forcibly, 'first of all, let's cut out the "Mr Strathern" bit—I'm sure the name Strathern has enough unhappy associations for you without you being reminded of them every time you address me.' If he saw her flinch, he ignored it. 'Secondly, let's omit the small talk and get down to business.'

The sheer force of his personality was like a dash of cold water in her face. 'To business?' she repeated faintly. 'What on earth are you talking about?'

'I'm not here just to make a pleasant social call, surely you realise that.'

'Then why are you here?' She leaned forward and her heavy dark hair fell about her face, framing the exquisite purity of her features. 'Rick——' she said sharply. 'Something's happened to Rick.'

'Rick, my dear girl, is flourishing as he always has and he always will. You still care about him, don't you?'

'I——' Her head bent so that her expression was hidden from him. 'I *was* engaged to him, after all.'

'Yes, you were engaged. And then after the accident, an accident for which he was responsible, he ditched you, didn't he?'

The brutal question hung in the air. Shannon reached down for her sherry, her jade green eyes staring into space, her hand shaking so violently that she knocked the glass sideways. The crystal rang as it struck the tray.

Her shoulders slumped in sudden despair. 'I'm always doing things like that,' she muttered.

'Because you're blind,' Blaise Strathern said brutally. 'That's what my precious brother did to you, isn't it? Because of his criminal carelessness, he caused the car accident that blinded you. And afterwards he didn't have the guts to stay around.'

She pressed the back of her hand against her mouth. 'How you hate him!' she exclaimed, appalled by the savagery in his voice.

'And so should you. But this evening, if I'd been Rick, you would have welcomed me with open arms, wouldn't you?'

'No!'

'Tell the truth, Shannon. I saw your face, remember?'

'Maybe I would have,' she retorted. 'But you're not Rick, are you? So none of this is really any of your business.'

'I'm making it my business.'

'What on earth for?'

'Because of you.'

His brief reply utterly frustrated her. 'You're talking in riddles,' she said rudely. 'I'm nothing to you, Blaise Strathern.'

'Maybe not now. But you're going to be.'

'Are you threatening me?' she said incredulously.

'If you choose to interpret it as such.'

'Look,' she said roundly, 'half an hour ago I didn't even know you existed, and I still don't know why you came here. But I do know this much—I dislike you already. I've never met anyone quite so rude and over-bearing as you in my whole life!'

'Good,' he said calmly. 'At least I got a reaction out of you. I was beginning to wonder if you had any spirit at all.'

She gasped with outrage, reaching down beside her chair for the little bell with which she summoned Bridget. He moved so quickly that she scarcely sensed his approach. The bell was wrested from her fingers. 'Don't do that,' he said evenly. 'I didn't come all the way from Quebec just to be shown the door.'

One hand was still around her wrist. She tried to pull it free, but her strength was only a travesty of his. Suddenly frightened, she felt her heartbeat quicken. Her mother was away, so she and Bridget were alone in the house. A middle-aged servant and a blind girl, alone with a man about whom they knew virtually nothing. His other hand fell on her shoulder and through the thin material of her dress she felt its warmth and its latent strength. 'Let go!' she said breathlessly.

'Don't be frightened, Shannon.' There was such gentleness in his voice that her brow furrowed in puzzlement. 'I had to find out, don't you see? I had to find out if there was any fight left in you. When I first walked in here and saw you, I thought perhaps I'd come too late.'

She shook her head helplessly. His hands were still holding her, and with the sharpened perception that had developed since the accident she knew he was very close to her; she could sense his body heat, hear the steady rhythm of his breathing, and it seemed impossible that he should not hear the irregular pounding of her own heart. She was suddenly achingly conscious of her loss of sight—if only she knew what he looked like! With what might have seemed like startling irrelevance to him, she said, 'Are you very tall?'

'Stand up and you'll see.'

She winced. 'Are you trying to be funny?'

He sounded genuinely puzzled. 'What do you mean?'

'Stand up and you'll *see*.'

'Oh . . . so what do you want me to do, Shannon? Use a special kind of vocabulary with you because you're blind? Avoid using all the words like "see" and "look" and "eyes"? You won't get concessions like that from me. As far as I'm concerned you're a normal young woman who happens to be blind and who's obviously using that as an excuse to let life pass her by—just don't expect me to encourage you, that's all.'

His bluntness, even though it angered her, was like a breath of fresh air. How often had her mother's friends subsided into an embarrassed silence when they had inadvertently used those words, with the result that Shannon herself had become morbidly over-sensitive to them. But Blaise Strathern was treating her just as he would treat anyone else. . . .

Holding herself straight, she slowly stood up. Her hands slid up his chest—he was wearing a silk shirt and what felt like a suede jacket—to his shoulders; her head, she guessed, would easily fit under his chin. 'You *are* tall,' she ventured.

'Six foot three, one hundred and eighty pounds.' A trace of laughter underlay his matter-of-fact words.

Shyly she smiled up at him and hazarded a guess. 'And you're an athlete.'

'Boxing, long-distance running and skiing.'

She began to laugh, and it seemed impossible that the green eyes glinting up at him could not see; it was his first glimpse of the Shannon of a year ago, the Shannon Rick had known. His startlingly blue eyes intent on the heart-shaped face with its creamy smooth skin and delicately flushed cheeks, he asked, 'Why are you laughing?'

'Just remind me to behave myself when I'm around you,' she teased. 'I'd be no match for you, that's for sure.'

She could not see the sudden fire in his eyes, nor the way his gaze lingered on her gentle, vulnerable mouth. 'You must know how beautiful you are,' he said roughly. 'That gives you an unfair advantage.'

She moved back fractionally. In a low voice she said, 'I can't think of myself as beautiful—not now.'

'Then you're a fool.'

'You don't mince your words, do you?'

'I rarely find it necessary to do so.'

He was as unlike his half brother as he could be, the girl thought, remembering with a pang Rick's easygoing charm and quick wit; Rick had never upbraided her or spoken to her harshly. Following her train of thought, she said, 'Do you look like Rick at all?'

'Some people say we look alike,' was the indifferent response. 'Same colouring—blond hair, blue eyes.'

She suppressed a sigh of frustration, for his laconic description was as good as worthless. Then she heard herself say, 'How is Rick? Have you seen him lately?'

'I saw him last week for the first time in several months—I've been away in France. I'd heard he'd got himself engaged, but I hadn't heard about the accident or its aftermath. When I finally got the information out of him, I booked a flight out here.'

They were back to the starting point. 'Why?' she said baldly.

'Evidently Rick was responsible for this.' Feather-light his fingers brushed her eyes with their fringe of dark, silky lashes. 'He walked away from that responsibility. As his older brother I felt I had to see you, to at least get an idea of how you've managed to come to terms with what happened. The minute I walked in that door, I knew I had a job on my hands.'

She retreated behind a mask of formality. 'That's where you're wrong, Mr Strathern,' she said coldly. 'There's nothing here for you to do. I'm fine as I am, and the last thing I need is the attentions of another well-meaning do-gooder.' The bitterness in her words surprised even herself; she had not realised the depth of her resentment against the legion of her mother's friends who had fluttered and cooed around her for the first few weeks and then gradually drifted away.

It was as though he had not heard her. 'When I

walked in this room I saw a young woman sitting alone in the darkness—doing nothing, just sitting.' He tweaked the sleeve of her dress contemptuously. 'Dowdily dressed, as pale as a ghost, needing the attentions of a hairdresser——'

'She usually comes to the house,' the girl retorted, stung. 'She hasn't been able to make it out here the last couple of weeks.'

'So why don't you go to her?'

'How can I?' she burst out. 'I tried going once, walking with a cane. I tripped and fell and had to be taken home in a taxi. It was utterly humiliating.'

'Your mother could take you.'

'She did, once. But she got so upset because people stared at us that she never would do it again.'

He expelled his breath in a tiny hiss. 'I see,' he said, and strangely enough Shannon felt as though he did see —beyond her words to the frustration and heartache of being always dependent on other people.

'Very well,' he went on briskly. 'Call up the hairdresser first thing tomorrow and get an appointment. I'll see that you get there and back safely. In the meantime I'll come tomorrow afternoon around two and take you out for a drive—we'll try and get some colour in your cheeks.'

Shannon braced herself against the chair. 'Mr Strathern——'

'Blaise.'

'Blaise, then. Listen, this has gone far enough, it's no longer even faintly amusing. Even if you did have an obligation to start with, and that's arguable, as far as I'm concerned you've fulfilled it. Since the accident——' momentarily her voice faltered, 'I've made a new life for myself. Maybe not a very exciting life by your standards, but then you're not the one who's blind, are you? So you can go home where you belong. And when next you see Rick, you can tell him I'm doing fine.

'I don't tell lies for anyone, Shannon.' Briefly there was the heaviness of his hand on her shoulder. 'Tomorrow at two. I'll let myself out.'

She opened her mouth to speak, but there was the diminishing fall of his footsteps across the carpet and then the click of the front door latch. A crunch of gravel, the roar of the motor, and he was gone. Her knees suddenly weak, Shannon sank back in the chair.

'Shannon, dearie, are you all right? I just heard Mr Strathern leave.'

'Yes, I'm fine, Bridget,' Shannon said, suppressing an almost hysterical urge to giggle: how many times this evening had she said she was fine? And to so little effect. . . .

'There now, you spilled your sherry,' Bridget clucked. 'It's been a long while since you've done that.' A pause. 'How did you get along with your visitor?'

Bridget had been with the Harts for as long as Shannon could remember. Officially she was called the maid, and even in these liberated days she still insisted on wearing an old-fashioned black uniform and a crisp white cap on her iron-grey curls, themselves as rigidly arranged as the rooms she tidied and dusted. But to Shannon she had always been a friend and confidante, for the fierce blue eyes concealed a heart as soft as butter. It was Bridget who had steered Shannon through those first dreadful days at home, who had insisted she learn how to feed herself and find her way around the house, who had cleaned up the inevitable spills and bathed the inevitable bruises.

'He says he's coming back tomorrow to take me out. I told him I didn't want to go, but I don't think he heard a word I said.'

'He looked like a man used to having his own way.'

'What *does* he look like, Bridget?'

Bridget sat down, for there was nothing she liked better than a cosy chat. 'A fine figure of a man,' she said warmly, with some of the lilt of her native Ireland in her voice. 'Well built, very tall. Thick hair, fair, but streaked by the sun. And his eyes ... blue as—as the sky on a summer's day,' she finished triumphantly.

Fascinated in spite of herself, Shannon asked, 'How old would you say he was?'

'Oh, perhaps in his mid-thirties. Very well dressed—there's obviously money there. When is he coming tomorrow?'

'Around two.'

'Then we'll have to see that your hair is washed, won't we? If it's a nice day you could wear that pretty beige suit.'

Apart from strolls in the garden, it was weeks since Shannon had been beyond the confines of the house, and she felt a quiver of mingled anticipation and fear. 'I'm scared of him, Bridget,' she said slowly. 'I don't understand what he wants of me.'

'Perhaps he just wants to take an attractive young woman for a drive,' Bridget suggested prosaically.

'I wish I could believe that. But I don't think it's that simple.'

'Time will tell, won't it, dearie?' said Bridget with the air of one pronouncing great wisdom. 'Do you need anything before you go to bed?'

'No, thanks.'

'I'll see you in the morning, then. And I'll press your suit for you first thing.'

Once again Shannon was left alone with her thoughts in the quiet room. The last time she had worn that suit she had been with Rick, she remembered painfully. It had been the first warm day of the spring, and after lunch they had strolled hand in hand along the waterfront of Victoria's inner harbour where the ferries and cruise boats were moored. The cherry trees and the tulips were in bloom and the air had been soft with the promise of summer, and because she was young and in love everything had seemed beautiful to her, touched with a magic golden glow.

She had met Rick the winter before, during her first term at the University of Victoria, where she was majoring in history. He had been giving a week-long series of lectures in economics; he was a senior executive and the tax consultant for a large corporation in Victoria. Because she had attended a private girls' school all through her teenage years, Shannon's experience of men was limited in the extreme, but during that first term it had become clear enough that her mother strongly disliked the young, jeans-clad, bearded students who were Shannon's contemporaries. So at first Rick Strathern with his tailored business suits and impeccable good manners had merely seemed a suitable escort to please her mother. The situation had changed very rapidly, however, for Rick's good looks, his sophistication, and his flattering pleasure in her company had soon gone to Shannon's head and before she knew it, she was in love with him. The sound of his voice on the telephone could fill a day with sunshine, while his kisses left her trembling. Delighted to please him, she pandered to his every whim; so there were no quarrels, no disappointments. Their courtship became a whirlwind of parties and restaurants and theatres, of excitement and fun, with no time to think or to look beneath the surface of their relationship. Certainly in her innocence Shannon had no inkling that his lovemaking was rather less frequent and less demanding than one might expect; instead she was naïvely grateful for his restraint.

They were to be married in August. In July they had taken the ferry from Vancouver Island to the mainland to visit some friends of Rick's in the Fraser Valley.

Because of the heavy traffic at the height of the tourist season, they were behind schedule, and Rick was driving very fast. If Shannon could be said to have any criticism of her fiancé, it would have been of his driving; more than once he had frightened her by his recklessness and his impatient disregard of other drivers' rights. That day, her hand resting on his knee, her green eyes anxious, she had remonstrated with him. 'It doesn't matter if we're a bit late, does it, Rick? You scared me when you passed that truck.'

'Yes, it does matter,' he said curtly. 'The Hudsons have invited another couple as well, Dick and Nancy Marling. Dick's the vice-president of Pacific Investments and he could be a valuable contact for me. I don't want to start off the weekend by being late—that's not the way to make a good impression.'

'I thought this was supposed to be a weekend away from work!'

'Honey, in my job you're never away from it. Some of my best deals have been made on weekends like this.'

'You mean your friends are chosen for their usefulness?' she asked in a small voice.

'That's putting it a bit bluntly, but essentially I suppose you're right.'

'But what about me—how am I useful to you?'

He had grinned down at her. He was driving with the windows down and the wind ruffled his soft, pale hair. 'You're too young and sweet to know what it's all about,' he teased. 'And that's why I love you.'

Shannon smiled uncertainly, knowing there was something she disliked in this conversation, but hesitant to put her finger on it. 'You must have had a lot of other girl-friends. . . .'

'Oh, a few, here and there,' he said airily, whipping around a sedan and squeezing ahead of it.

'Were they like me?'

'Good God, no—they knew the score, they'd all been around. That's why I want to marry you, Shannon— because you're different.'

With this she had to be content. She folded her hands in her lap, and the miles sped by. Another twenty minutes and they would be there ... the road was narrower now, winding through the hills, while behind them the sun was sinking downwards towards the rough-hewn peaks of the Rocky Mountains. They careered up another hill. Rick muttered something uncomplimentary under his breath about the driver ahead of them, flicked a glance at his rear view mirror and pulled over into the left-hand lane to pass the offending car.

Towards them over the crest of the hill came a transport truck, blue smoke puffing from its twin exhaust pipes. There was the blare of its horn. The unforgettable image of thousands of pounds of steel and chrome and rubber bearing down on them. The driver's face, a rictus of horror.

Rick swerved with a scream of tyres, but he was too late. The truck caught the left fender and for Shannon the world exploded into the screech of tortured metal and a shattering impact that mercifully blotted out her consciousness . . . .

The next few days were never anything but a blur in her memory. Blackness. Pain. The garbled sound of voices, remote and unreal.

It was five days after the accident that she fully came to herself. She lay still, puzzled and frightened. Where was she? Why was it so dark? There was something soft and constricting over her eyes and when she tried to open them, she could not. In sudden panic she cried out, 'Please—where am I?'

And then the nightmare began—a nightmare from which she would not wake up. Soothing feminine voices telling her everything was all right, when she knew it was not; the deeper voice of a doctor, his words an amalgam of horror: severe concussion, damage to the optic nerve, fortunately no external scarring, perhaps an operation in a year or so . . . and finally the word itself. Blindness. . . .

People came and went. Her mother and the nurses; her regular doctor, interns and specialists. So it was almost a week before Shannon had the courage to ask her mother the question that had been tormenting her. 'Why hasn't Rick been to see me yet?' That he had not been seriously hurt in the accident she had ascertained some time ago.

There was a perceptible pause. Already Shannon was becoming more adept at distinguishing nuances from people's voices, and it was no trouble to sense the evasiveness when her mother spoke. 'He thought you'd need time to get over the initial shock, darling. As you know, he had only had a few stitches in one hand and slight bruising, so he was discharged from hospital the next day. I believe he was able to visit his friends briefly after all.' The all-important business deal, Shannon thought, with a bitterness new to her. 'But then he had to fly back to Victoria. He couldn't very well stay here. He'll be in to see you on the weekend, though, I'm sure.'

The days dragged by and finally it was Friday evening, then Saturday. It was not until Sunday afternoon that Shannon heard the familiar light step coming along the corridor to her room. She lay quietly, her heart beating in great sickening thumps. The footsteps stopped. When she could stand the silence no longer she called out, 'Rick? Is that you?'

'Hi there, honey.' A brush of lips on her forehead. A huge bouquet was put beside her, fern tickling her cheek and the heavy scent of carnations filling her nostrils.

'They smell lovely,' she said falsely. 'Thank you.'

'How are you feeling?'

Her useless eyes strained to pierce the bandages. 'Okay, I guess. The headaches aren't as bad any more. They say I can get up in a couple of days.'

'Great! You'll be home in no time, I expect.'

'Yes.' Frantically she sought for something to say. 'Are you back at work?'

'I had to go back almost immediately—we're busier than we've ever been with the new Stanway contract and the possibility of getting Marsden's company to amalgamate with us. . . .' He went on and on, and after a while she stopped listening. But then her attention was jerked back. '. . . so I think we should delay it for a while, don't you, honey?'

'What?' she said stupidly. 'Delay what?'

'Our wedding—weren't you listening?'

She felt very cold. 'Delay it until when?'

'Just for a while until we see how things go. I don't think we should rush into anything, do you?'

She gathered her courage. 'Rick, are you saying you don't want to marry me?'

'No, of course not!' he snapped irritably. 'I don't think you were listening, Shannon. I merely said we should wait a while. Until the fall maybe.'

'A blind wife is more than you bargained for,' she said with brutal honesty.

He took her flaccid fingers in his. 'I love you, Shannon,' he said over-loudly. 'But we have to be sensible and allow ourselves time to adjust to this—this difficulty.'

Her lips twisted. 'Yes,' she said stonily, 'I suppose you're right.'

'Oh, here's the nurse,' said Rick with such transparent relief that Shannon did not know whether to laugh or cry. 'I'll get her to put the flowers in a vase. Do you like them, hon?'

'They're beautiful,' she said, and not even all her will-power could keep the tension and weariness from her voice.

The nurse said cheerfully, 'Tired, Miss Hart?'

Shannon nodded dumbly, unsurprised to hear Rick say, 'I'd better be going then, Shannon. My plane leaves early this evening.' He squeezed her hand and gave her a brisk kiss.

Forgetting her pride, she said, 'Will you be able to come and see me again?'

'Sure I will. I'll be in touch. Take care of yourself, honey.'

As if she had any choice. . . . The nurse fussed around her for what seemed an intolerably long time and then finally, blessedly, she was alone and could surrender to the black despair that had been her constant companion for so many days.

True to his word, Rick did come again. But it was not until Shannon's last day at the hospital, when she had almost given up hope. She was dressed and sitting in the chair by the window, waiting for her mother to come and drive her home, when she heard the familiar steps come into her room. Her head swung around. 'Rick!' she exclaimed, 'I'm *so* glad you're here. How are you?'

'I'm fine. Going home today, eh? You must be excited.'

She was not. In the past weeks the hospital had become like home, its rules and routines familiar and comforting; to leave it and venture into the unknown world filled her with dread. Out there she would no longer have the anonymity of being just another patient; she would be different, abnormal, no longer one of the crowd. No, she was not excited: she was terrified. But something warned her against sharing this with Rick. 'Now that you're here, we can all go home together,' she said lightly.

'I—I'm afraid that's not possible.'

Unconsciously her hands clenched in her lap as all

her doubts of the past weeks crystallised into a fatalistic sense of doom. She stared at him with her beautiful blind eyes, unable to see how his own eyes fell. 'Something's wrong, isn't it, Rick?' she said quietly. 'You'd better tell me about it.'

'I've been transferred to the east coast,' he said flatly. 'I leave next week. It's a big promotion for me and I certainly can't afford to turn it down.'

He fell silent. She waited, her mouth dry. 'Well,' he finally burst out, 'aren't you going to congratulate me?'

She felt like an animal caught in a trap, waiting for the death blow to descend. 'If the job is what you want, then I'm pleased for you,' she said carefully.

'You're not making this any easier, are you?' he demanded angrily. 'I can't marry you, Shannon. You must see that it's impossible now. I'll be doing a lot of travelling, a lot of entertaining—you wouldn't feel comfortable with that kind of life-style.'

Mercifully an answering anger began to burn its way along her veins. 'Speak for yourself, Rick, not for me,' she said sharply. 'What you mean is, you don't want a blind wife.'

'It wouldn't be fair of me to marry you—it would be making too many demands on you.'

'Don't be so sickeningly high-minded!' she cried, throwing away the last vestiges of control. 'What you mean is, I'd cramp your style the way I am now. I'd be a nuisance, a handicap. Ambitious young executives marry normal healthy women, don't they? Not someone like me.'

'You're putting the worst possible interpretation on my behaviour——'

'It's the *only* possible interpretation, isn't it?' Wearily, feeling the beginnings of a headache, she rubbed her forehead. 'I think you'd better go, Rick. This isn't getting us anywhere.'

'Look, Shannon, I'm sorry——'

She could see him as clearly in her mind as if through her eyes: his fine drawn face with its flat cheekbones and straight, tightly held mouth; his light blue eyes that had so often smiled into hers; his slim, narrow-shouldered body no doubt immaculately dressed.

'Please, Rick, I'd like you to go now,' she repeated. She had lost weight since the accident and it was no trouble to slip his ring, a circlet of sparkling diamonds, off her finger. She held it out and mercifully her hand was steady.

'Keep it? I——'

'No, I want you to have it.' She was nearing the end of her endurance and it took all her strength to keep her voice as steady as her hand. 'Goodbye, Rick.'

The ring was plucked from her palm, he muttered something inaudible, and then she heard him leave the room. She huddled into the chair, pressing her ice-cold fingers against her mouth to hold back the choking sobs that, once started, she would be unable to stop. To the physical darkness in which she daily moved and breathed was now added an inner darkness, the devastating loneliness that was betrayal and the loss of love. . . .

Slowly Shannon came back to the present. The room was cooler now and she became aware that she was bone tired. She stood up and made her way to the door; she had memorised the position of every piece of furniture, every stair and doorway in the house, and could move about with deceptive ease. Automatically as she left the room she flipped off the light switch. Up the stairs (eighteen of them), past the homely tick of the grandfather clock, down the hallway ten paces to her bedroom. In the darkness she began to undress, folding her clothes carefully so that she would have no trouble finding them in the morning. Her nightdress was under her pillow.

Slipping it over her head, she got into bed. Strangely enough, after recollecting so clearly those last times with Rick, it was not Rick of whom she was thinking as she drifted off to sleep. Instead it was the harsh-voiced stranger, with his firm grip and abrasive honesty, who filled her mind. If she allowed him to, he would change her life, disrupt its safe, placid routine and tear away the protective shell she had so laboriously grown over her emotions and over the wounds of the past. Acceptance of her disability had come too hard to allow anyone to do that. Tomorrow, she thought drowsily, she would tell him she did not want to see him again. Tomorrow she would tell him. . . .

CHAPTER TWO

IT was not to be that simple. It was immediately obvious the next day that Bridget was on the stranger's side, for Shannon's suit was pressed and her shoes polished before the girl even got up. 'After your shower I'll dry your hair and curl it loosely. It looks very nice like that,' said Bridget as she deposited the early morning cup of tea by Shannon's bed.

'Bridget, I'm not going to go out with him. I've decided I don't want to. I'm sorry you've already pressed the suit—you could have saved yourself the trouble.'

'Nonsense! A fine-looking man like that? Of course you're going out with him.'

'I'm not,' Shannon persisted stubbornly. 'I hate going out. I always feel as though everybody's staring at me. And you know how I fell that time and had to come home in a taxi. I won't do it, Bridget.'

'Mr Strathern may have something to say about that.'

'He can say what he likes. Short of dragging me out by brute force, he can't make me do anything I don't want to do.'

'Maybe so, maybe not,' Bridget said enigmatically. 'At any rate, there's no harm in you looking nice—that suit is very becoming, and even if you don't want to go out, maybe he'll stay for a cup of tea.'

Blaise Strathern had not struck Shannon as the type of man to sit around drinking tea and making polite conversation, but she forebore to say so. Anyway, maybe Bridget was right—it would be good for her own morale to know she looked her best and it would give her the self-confidence she would need to oppose her visitor's wishes.

Promptly at two the doorbell rang. Shannon was upstairs, her fingers methodically sorting through the contents of her drawer to find her perfume, and in spite of her intention to remain calm and in control, she felt her nerve ends quiver. Hurriedly she sprayed her wrists and throat, then moved towards the door. As Blaise Strathern entered the hall, she began descending the stairs, her slim, ringless fingers sliding down the banister, her face intent on making no mistakes. He watched her in silence, his eyes narrowed, his expression unreadable.

Today she looked very different. Her hair, the colour of polished mahogany, fell in shining waves to her shoulders; make-up subtly enhanced the brilliant almond-shaped eyes, the high cheekbones and softly curving mouth. Her suit had a Chanel-type jacket over a jade silk blouse, with a small-waisted, gathered skirt, while delicate high-heeled shoes emphasised the fragility of ankle and foot. She reached the bottom step and perhaps only he noticed the faintest hesitation before she moved across the carpet in his direction, her hand outstretched. 'Mr Strathern?'

He took her hand and she felt it being raised to his

lips and then a touch like fire on her skin. Tensing, she tried to pull free, all her senses warning her of danger. Her head turned as she heard the retreat of Bridget's footsteps. 'Bridget——'

'I'm expecting the paper boy, dear, I'd better wait for him in the kitchen.'

Feeling very much alone, Shannon licked her lips nervously; she had counted on Bridget's presence for support.

'Are you ready?'

There seemed no point in prevaricating. 'I'm not going.'

'So that's the way the wind blows, is it? You got all dressed up—and very nice you look, too—just to give yourself the courage to tell me to get lost.'

She blushed, for it was the exact truth. 'I don't want to go out with you. I can't see that it will serve any useful purpose.'

'That's where you're wrong, my dear. Come along, it's a beautiful day, we'll go for a drive first and then I'll take you somewhere for tea.'

Ineffectually she tried to free her hand. 'You're not listening to me! I've said no——'

'Shannon, you're not going to win this one. So you might as well give in gracefully.'

'I don't think you're used to a woman saying no to you!'

'You may well be right.' There was lazy amusement in the deep voice. 'Be that as it may, you're coming with me, Shannon, if I have to pick you up and carry you out to the car.' His hands swiftly encircled her waist and instinctively she raised her palms to push him away. But before she could protest, he said coaxingly, 'Please, Shannon—the sun is shining, it's spring time, and I would enjoy your company.'

Her breath seemed to have caught in her throat. When

he was being dictatorial she had no compunction in fighting him, but against his pleading she was helpless. She capitulated with rather poor grace. 'All right. Is my handbag here somewhere?'

'On the table. I'll get it.'

He slipped a casual hand under her arm as they went down the front steps and along the neatly gravelled path that led between beds of yellow tulips and sweetly scented narcissus; guiding her around the car, he helped her into the seat. A few seconds later he slid in beside her, turning on the ignition and circling the big rosebed in front of the house before following the quarter-mile-long curve of the driveway through the overhanging trees to the road. 'I thought we'd drive north. There's a rather pleasant provincial park not far from Sidney.'

With studied rudeness she said, 'For very obvious reasons it really doesn't matter to me where we go.'

'I'm glad you said that,' was the unexpected reply. 'Because it brings it all out into the open, doesn't it? It's been a long time since I've met anyone quite so determined to be miserable as you.'

'That's a dreadful thing to say!'

'Is it? You stop and think about it for a minute. And then give me some honest answers to the questions I want to ask you.'

She turned her face towards him, pink patches of temper in her cheeks. 'You want me to behave as though there's absolutely nothing wrong with me, don't you? They assured me in the hospital that I looked just the same as I did before the accident, so I suppose it doesn't show that I'm blind. Except when I trip over things or spill my food or can't move out of the house unless someone goes with me. I'm blind, Blaise Strathern —so stop treating me as though all I've got is a cut finger!'

'I know you're blind! So are thousands of other

people. A lot of them older than you, and certainly not as well off as you. They aren't sitting home feeling sorry for themselves. They've got jobs, they've learned to read Braille, they've got seeing-eye dogs instead of white canes——'

Childishly she interrupted him. 'My mother would never tolerate a dog in the house.'

'—and they're not sitting home feeling sorry for themselves.'

In the hospital Shannon had planned to learn Braille once she was home, and had determined to make herself as independent as possible. But then Rick had left her life, taking with him laughter and love and shared hopes. And somehow her mother had always had a good reason to delay any visits to the local institute for the blind, while Shannon's tentative mention of a dog had met with icy refusal. Slowly, imperceptibly, the days had begun to merge into one another, each no different from any of the rest, and equally imperceptibly the safety and comfort of the house had become more important than any of Shannon's uncertain and tentative attempts to assert herself.

She twisted her hands in her lap, her head bent, for the first time in many days realising the extent of her isolation from the normal world, and, equally, the extent to which she had fallen short of those first, ambitious plans.

Perhaps something showed in her face. At any rate the man sitting beside her reached over and patted her hand, saying more gently, 'You let yourself get into a rut, didn't you? Without even realising quite how it happened. . . .'

'I guess you're right,' she said with the innate honesty that was one of her basic traits.

'Acknowledging the problem is the first step towards solving it.'

She did not even notice that she used his first name. 'Blaise, that's all very well, but essentially there is no solution.'

'Do you want to continue the way you are?'

'No!' The force behind the word shocked her. 'But I don't have much choice,' she finished lamely.

'You were part way through university when this happened, weren't you?'

'Yes.'

'Learn Braille, get a guide dog, and go back and finish your degree.'

'You make it sound so absurdly simple!'

'Of course it's not simple, Shannon. But it can be done.'

She sat quietly, her brow furrowed, and sensibly Blaise remained silent. 'I was majoring in history,' she said eventually.

'I didn't know that. I'm a combination historian and archaeologist myself. Doing research on the early French settlements in Quebec at the moment—hence the year in France.'

Her face lit up and she began asking questions that were both enthusiastic and intelligent, all her earlier antagonism forgotten. The time passed quickly and before she knew it, Blaise had pulled into a side road and parked the car. He got out, came round and opened her door. 'There's a picnic bench just a few feet away. Let's go and sit down.'

He steered her unobtrusively to the bench. 'From where I'm sitting,' he said conversationally, 'I can see the Gulf Islands in the strait and in the distance the peaks of the mountains in Washington. There's a beach below us and the arbutus trees are in leaf. The sea is a brilliant clear blue, bluer than the sky.'

'Bridget told me your eyes were the colour of a summer sky.'

For the first time in their brief acquaintance she sensed

he was disconcerted. 'Well—they *are* blue.'

She smiled mischievously, the sea wind tugging at her hair. 'I do believe I've embarrassed you.'

He laughed, a warm, relaxed, very masculine sound. 'You'll never get me to admit that.'

Above her head a squirrel scolded among the pines while a pair of chickadees called back and forth before flying away in a whirr of wings. The sun was warm on Shannon's face; the tang of salt water filled her nostrils, clean and sweet and pure. 'Thank you for bringing me, Blaise,' she said slowly. 'I'm enjoying being here.'

'My pleasure, Shannon.'

He was sitting close to her. 'What are you wearing?' she asked, wanting to visualise him in her mind.

'Beige trousers and a blue crewneck sweater under a brown corduroy jacket.'

Tentatively she raised one hand. 'I'd like to have a better idea of what you look like. Do you mind if I touch you?'

'Not at all.'

The squirrel had gone away and there was only the sighing of the wind in the pine boughs. Closing her eyes in concentration, Shannon brought both hands up to his face and her fingers began a delicate, feather-light exploration. His hair was thick and soft, with a slight tendency to curl. His eyes were deep set, and the planes of his face too strong and angular for classic good looks, the chin below the straight nose too determined. She was finding it hard to maintain her composure, for there was something peculiarly intimate in the brush of her fingertips over his skin. She found his mouth and momentarily her hand lingered.

The quickened breathing she could hear, but she had no idea of the self-control he was exercising to remain immobile under her touch. Abruptly she dropped her hands to her lap. 'Thank you,' she said breathlessly.

'Shannon, is there no hope that you'll ever get your sight back?'

'In the hospital there was mention of the chance of an operation in a year or so's time. But Dr Snider, who's our family doctor, says there's no chance of recovery and I'd be foolish to even consider surgery.'

'I see.' A grimness in his voice. 'Let's go and find some tea, shall we?'

Her brief serenity fled. Knowing she had to tell the truth, she said miserably, 'Blaise, I'm scared to death of restaurants. I went once with my mother and some of her friends and it was just awful. I'd really rather go home instead. Bridget would make us some tea.'

'No, Shannon. You're through with running away. Believe me, it will be different when you're with me.' She felt the weight of his hands rest on her shoulders. 'I want you to trust me. I'll be right beside you all the time. I won't let you fall, or spill anything, or in any way humiliate yourself. If you'll just depend on me to look after you, no one even need know you're blind.'

If only she could believe him. . . . 'I—I have this nightmare sometimes,' she confessed, and briefly her forehead rested on his shoulder, her hair tumbling over his chest. 'I've been taken to a restaurant and then suddenly the person I'm with disappears and the waiters are jostling me, and gradually all the people at the tables stop talking because they're all staring at me, and I have no idea which way to go or what's in front of me. . . .' She was trembling slightly, for in describing it, the nightmare was as vivid as reality.

His arm went around her, holding her close. 'I'll never do that to you, Shannon, never. Trust me.'

Her cheek was against his sweater and she could feel the slow, steady beat of his heart. She had not been held like this for nearly a year, not since Rick had gone away. It was at the same time comforting and secure, yet disturbing and strangely frightening. Part of her knew she should break free of his embrace; part of her wanted to remain there; but a third part acknowledged the urge to slide her hands under his jacket and hold him closer, to raise her face to be kissed . . . and this part, to her horror, was far stronger than the other two.

She pushed back against his chest with her palms. She had trusted Rick, she thought wildly. And now she was being asked to trust his half-brother, who, she already knew, was a far more-complex and subtle man than Rick would ever be. 'I'd rather go home,' she reiterated stubbornly.

'You know what you're saying, don't you? You're saying safety is more important than risk, the known more important than the unknown. You're turning your back on the world, Shannon. Is that really what you want—to spend the rest of your days closeted in that house, with only Bridget and your mother for company? You're young, you're beautiful, and you could be very much alive . . . the choice is yours.'

Battered by his words, in her heart knowing them to be true, Shannon fought for composure. The wind had freshened and from the ruffled waters of the strait came the wild, mournful cry of a sea gull.

He was speaking again. 'I'm perfectly capable of picking you up bodily and forcing you to go to that restaurant, you know as well as I do. But I won't do that, Shannon. As I said a minute ago, the choice has to be yours. Just think carefully before you make it. Because if you say, "No, take me home," I shall obey you. And this evening I'll get the night flight back to Quebec and you won't hear from me again. But if you say, "Yes"—then I'll do everything in my power to help you become an independent, whole person again.'

He was no longer touching her. In fact, she sensed he had moved away from her, putting a physical distance between them. She was equally sure he had said all he was going to say. The choice was indeed hers. She could run for shelter like a terrified animal, cowering beneath the shadows of her mother's over-protection and Bridget's care. Or she could step out into the sunlight and the wind, and face the perils and joys of life in the open.

In one of those odd tricks that the mind can play, she found herself catapulted into the past. She could remember very little of her father, who had died before she was five, but one of the memories she had always treasured was of his teaching her to ride a two-wheel bike. It had been a sunny day, very like today, and he had been running beside her, holding on to the saddle to help her keep her balance. Then he had let go and all alone she had wobbled precariously along the driveway, knowing he would catch her if she fell, but knowing also, and proudly, that he thought she could manage by herself. Her father would never have spent ten months sitting in a quiet house, defeated and lonely and bored. Her father, she recognised instinctively, would have liked Blaise Strathern. . . .

She raised her head, a defiant tilt to her chin. Without conscious thought the words came from deep within her. 'Please will you take me to the restaurant, Blaise?'

'I will be very happy to do so,' he said formally.

A simple request and a simple answer. Yet they were words that would change her life, Shannon knew. She realised too that Blaise Strathern understood as well as she all that had not been said. Hands took hers and raised her to her feet. 'Ready?' he said lightly.

'Ready!' she answered, and suddenly they were both laughing. His arm around her waist, he led her back to the car.

Fifteen minutes later he pulled off the main road up a slight slope and brought the car to a stop. 'This used to be the family home of one of the lumber barons, but it's a small hotel now. A delightful place, lovely gardens and good food.'

As she waited for him to help her out of the car, Shannon felt her nerves tighten with apprehension. She had to go through with this now, it was too late to change her mind, but she could not think of it as anything but an ordeal. Blaise must have read her mind, for as he opened her door he remarked, 'Relax, Shannon, we're doing this for enjoyment, remember?'

'It doesn't feel much like that to me,' she said ruefully.

He pulled her to her feet, and one arm remained around her waist. 'You're a beautiful young woman who's with a man who finds you most attractive, and it's springtime, and anyone who sees you looking the way you do now will never realise you're blind—they'll be too busy envying me for being your escort.'

She couldn't help smiling. 'That's pure flattery!'

'And if you keep smiling at me like that, and I keep my arm around you, which I shall, they'll be convinced we're in love.'

'Oh.' Oddly disconcerted, Shannon could find nothing to say. Her whole body was tinglingly aware of him beside her as she felt him guide her across the paved parking lot. He gave her low-voiced instructions about the front steps, which she negotiated without any trouble, and then they were inside. The hostess welcomed them warmly, obviously noticing nothing amiss.

'A table by the window, please,' said Blaise, then his head bent to Shannon's, his breath fanning her cheek. 'All right, darling?'

Her face flushed, her body curved to his, Shannon said lightly, 'Of course!' Warm lips brushed her cheek and the shock of this unexpected caress drove everything else from her mind. With lissome grace she moved beside him to the window and sat down at their table, her hands unobtrusively locating the edge of the table and the arms of the chair. With exquisite tact Blaise helped her choose from the menu and, when the food came, Shannon was surprised to find herself genuinely hungry. Dainty sandwiches and cakes served on delicate bone china. . . . 'This doesn't seem quite the right fare for you!' she chuckled.

'Next time I'll take you out for dinner. You should see what I can do to a steak! By the way, when's your hair appointment?'

'Tomorrow morning at ten.'

'Good. I'll pick you up at nine-thirty. I have tickets for the symphony tomorrow night, and afterwards we'll have dinner at Pierrots.'

Shannon had the feeling she was on a roller coaster that was carrying her faster and faster down a steep slope. 'You're going to far too much trouble,' she protested.

'Let me decide that. Are you ready to go?'

'Yes, thank you,' she said politely, her expression puzzled and uncertain.

He guided her to the foyer, paid the bill and led her outdoors again across the pavement. 'This isn't the way to the car,' Shannon said, tugging at Blaise's arm.

'I want to show you the garden.'

A latch clicked and then her heels were sinking into the grass and her nostrils were filled with the scent of blossoms. 'The cherry and plum trees are in bloom,' Blaise said softly. 'Against the far hedge there's a rockery with dwarf tulips and dark velvety wallflowers and tiny blue forget-me-nots.'

No wind here, only the drowsy humming of bees and the mingled fragrance of the flowers. A branch brushed Shannon's shoulder and she traced the rough bark and the double-frilled petals with her fingers, knowing she had to ask him the question that was on the tip of her tongue, yet reluctant to disturb the peace and tranquility of the garden. 'Blaise, why are you doing all this? Spending so much time with me, taking me to restaurants and concerts? I don't understand.'

'I already told you one reason—after Rick described what had happened to you as a result of the accident, as his older brother I felt I had to come and see how you were managing.'

She bit her lip, having no idea how provocative she looked with her pink cheeks reflecting the pink of the blossoms, her eyes as vivid as the green grass. 'So I'm a duty to you? An obligation? Is that it?'

'Initially that was it, yes.'

She frowned, wishing she could see his face. 'You feel sorry for me,' she accused. The branch in her fingers suddenly snapped. 'I hate that!' she said passionately. 'I can't bear to think of people pitying me.'

'You're jumping to all the wrong conclusions, Shannon. I never said I pitied you—nor is that why I am spending time with you.'

'Then *why*?'

'This is the reason,' he said grimly.

She felt herself being seized and pulled towards him and instinctively she stiffened in recoil. But her strength was nothing to his. Crushed against his chest, she felt fingers dig into her chin, raising her face. His mouth covered hers and the serenity of the garden vanished as if it had never been. Whimpering in her throat, she tried to pull away, but the bruising hold of his mouth only deepened until she was powerless to resist. Stormed by sensations she had never known existed, her heart a frantic tattoo in her breast, Shannon sagged against him, knowing that if he let go, she would fall.

So abruptly that a cry of protest was wrenched from her lips, he thrust her away, his fingers around her arms as cruel as the talons of a hawk. She could not see the blue blaze of his eyes. But his heartbeat had echoed her own, and in the quiet air, his breathing was ragged and harsh. 'That's why,' he grated. 'You didn't even guess, did you, my beautiful Shannon?'

Primitive terror struck her to the heart. 'I'm not your Shannon!'

As though she had not spoken, he said, 'You had no idea that I've been wanting to do that ever since I first saw you.'

'You're crazy,' she whispered. 'Twenty-four hours ago you hadn't even met me.'

'True enough—twenty-four hours ago you were just Rick's ex-fiancée. I hadn't even seen a picture of you.'

'I gave him one.' The words were torn from her.

'Then either he got rid of it, or he was lying when he told me he didn't have one.'

That Rick had not even cared enough about her to keep her picture seemed the final betrayal. Under the hard blue gaze of the man holding her, Shannon seemed to shrink. He said roughly, 'Rick's in the past, Shannon. I know you imagined yourself in love with him——'

'Imagined!' she interrupted furiously, tossing back her hair. 'I *was* in love with him——'

'Did he ever make you feel the way you did a minute ago when you were in my arms?'

He had not, of course, but she was not yet ready to admit that. 'Rick was gentle and kind,' she retorted. 'I wouldn't have tolerated him kissing me the way you did.'

'Oh?' Blaise said silkily. 'Then let's try this.' His body came between her and the sun and his shadow over her was like an omen. But his kiss was gentle and sure and his hands drifted from her shoulders along the slender length of her neck to bury themselves in the shining fall of her hair. His lips left hers, tracing her closed eyes, the smooth line of her cheekbone, before returning again to drink deep of her mouth.

She was helpless against his confident, intimate invasion, all her defences gone. Shyly, daringly, her lips moved against his, parting to the probing of his like petals opening in the sun. His arms gathered her to him, and her own arms slid around his neck as for the second time she felt the silky thickness of his hair. As drugged as the drowsy bees, she surrendered herself to the sweetness of a kiss that seemed to go on for ever.

It was Blaise who ended it. His words brought her back to her senses, words that fell like hailstones from a summer sky. 'Rick never kissed you like that either, did he?'

She fought for control, her cheeks very pale. 'This has all been a game to you, hasn't it?' she cried bitterly. 'You may have a degree of sexual experience that Rick lacked, Blaise Strathern, but I wouldn't have thought you were so naïve as to confuse that with love. I *loved* Rick.'

'Perhaps it would be more accurate if you were to rephrase that in the present tense,' he said viciously. 'He's not worth it, Shannon—he never was and he never will be. You, of all people, should know that.'

It was true that Rick had abandoned her when she needed him most. Somehow she had never been able to equate his action with the Rick she had loved, and over the past few months this had coalesced into the conviction that there must have been some reason she knew nothing about to account for his behaviour. To admit that he had heartlessly abandoned her because of her blindness would have been to admit that their love had been a sham, a mockery of truth. And that she had been unable to do.

With uncanny perception, Blaise added, 'And don't try and find excuses for him. There aren't any.'

'You don't know that!'

'So you persist in defending him—that speaks for itself, doesn't it, Shannon?' He took her by the elbow, his grip as impersonal as a stranger's. 'There's not much point in continuing this conversation. Come on.'

Stumbling a little on the grass, she followed him past the blossom-laden trees to the gate, and back to the car. He drove much more rapidly on the way home—as though he could not wait to be rid of her, she thought miserably, unable to think of anything to break the silence between them. Finally they turned into the driveway of her mother's house, and he pulled to a halt. On the front steps, about to press the doorbell, he said coldly, 'I'll pick you up at nine-thirty tomorrow morning.'

With equal coldness she replied, 'Please don't bother. I can get a taxi.'

'Unlike Rick, I don't go back on my word—I've said I'll take you, and I will.'

To argue would have been the equivalent of beating her head against a brick wall, she knew. 'Whatever you say.'

Her assumed meekness did not deceive him. 'You're rather overdoing it, my dear,' he said lazily. 'By the way, there's one other thing—one way or another I'm going to make you forget Rick.' A quick, hard kiss on her lips. His footsteps ran down the steps as behind her Bridget opened the door.

CHAPTER THREE

BRIDGET was cleaning the downstairs hall when the doorbell rang the next day. 'Good morning, Mr Strathern, come away in. Shannon's upstairs, I believe. I'll get her.'

But Shannon had been waiting in the dining room, waiting with a degree of anticipation that had faintly horrified her. She came quickly through the doorway, wearing thin-strapped sandals and a flowered peasant skirt with an embroidered cotton blouse. Just the sound of Blaise's voice as he returned Bridget's greeting had been enough to bring a faint flush to her cheeks and she was trying to hold herself with more confidence as she came around the corner; it seemed important that she erase from his mind that image of a dowdy girl sitting in the dark. Bridget's warning came just too late. Shannon's foot hit the vacuum cleaner and she pitched forward with a cry of fear. But instead of striking the floor, she cannoned against a man's hard chest and arms like steel bands brought her to her feet. Against her cheek she could feel the pounding of his heart and from his voice she knew he had been shaken by her near-fall. 'Are you all right?'

She nodded wordlessly. The brief incident epitomised for her the worst part of her handicap—the total unexpectedness with which accidents could happen; she was glad to remain still for a moment, his arms a haven, if only a temporary one.

'Shannon dearie, I'm so sorry,' Bridget was repeating tearfully. 'I thought you were upstairs, otherwise I'd never have left the wretched machine there.'

'It couldn't be helped, Bridget, and there's no harm done,' Blaise said authoritatively, and Shannon was amused to hear Bridget's meek, 'I suppose you're right, sir,' knowing that without Blaise's intervention, Bridget would have been berating herself for another ten minutes.

'We'd better go, Shannon, if your appointment's at ten.'

'Yes. Goodbye, Bridget, and don't worry, I'm really all right.'

Blaise's hand on her elbow, Shannon went down the front steps. It was a sunny day again, she thought appreciatively, taking a deep breath of the fresh spring air. The breeze tugged at her hair and blew the hem of her skirt around her knees. 'It's good to be outdoors,' she said spontaneously, smiling up at her companion, and just as spontaneously she heard herself add, 'Blaise, I know we quarrelled yesterday, but I would like you to know how much I appreciate your kindness to me—whatever the motive may be.'

'My pleasure,' he said drily. As they drove off, he went on, 'I made a couple of phone calls this morning. You can take lessons in Braille downtown on weekdays. And I've put your name on the waiting list for a guide dog.'

'You certainly believe in trying to run my life,' she said spiritedly.

'Someone has to—it's fairly obvious you weren't doing it yourself.'

She compressed her lips, knowing he was speaking the truth. 'Blaise, my mother will never let me have a dog!'

'This isn't an ordinary dog——'

'That won't make any difference.'

'It could give you a whole new life-style—your mother can't possibly object to that. As a very small example, there's no way you would have fallen this morning if you'd had a dog.'

Her head bent, her fingers twisting in her lap, she repeated dully, 'She won't let me, I know.'

'We'll see. Why haven't I met her yet, by the way—is she away?'

'Yes, she went to visit friends in California. She should be back tomorrow afternoon.'

'I see. You should start doing some regular physical exercises, Shannon—you have to be very fit to handle one of those dogs.'

She sighed, knowing it was hopeless. Her mother, for all her appearance of fragile femininity, had a will o iron, as Shannon had more than once discovered to her cost, and while it was fascinating to think of the difference

a guide dog could make to her life, it was useless specu-
lation, she was sure. But at least she could enjoy today,
she thought philosophically. Her mother could not spoil
today. . . .

It seemed as though nothing could spoil the day. The
hairdresser trimmed her hair, then wove it into a loose
knot on her crown, a style that subtly called attention to
the purity of Shannon's profile and her narrow, elegant
neck. Afterwards, she and Blaise strolled arm in arm
down the busy sidewalk to an outdoor café, where they
drank coffee and amiably discussed their favourite poets
and composers. The afternoon Shannon spent at home;
the evening passed by in a daze of delight. Whatever else
she might fault in Blaise Strathern, she could not criticise
his care of her; by now she trusted in this implicitly, and
consequently she was able to walk proudly at his side,
her long skirts rustling as she obeyed his occasional low-
voiced instruction. The music delighted her and sharing
in the audience's enthusiastic response made her feel reassuringly normal, part of the crowd. After the concert
they ate Pacific salmon and crêpes, the wine loosening
Shannon's tongue from its usual reticence so that she
gave Blaise a far clearer picture of her normal home life
than she realised. Then, finally, it was time to go home.
Blaise pulled up in front of the house and turned off the
ignition.

Shyly Shannon rested a hand on his arm. 'Thank you
for a wonderful evening, Blaise—I have enjoyed myself.
And thank you for taking care of me so well.'

His hand came down on hers, the lean, hard fingers
gently stroking her wrist. 'I enjoyed myself too, Shannon,' he said seriously. 'You're a delight to be with—
fresh, spontaneous, unaffected. And I find when I try
and describe things to you, I'm seeing them myself
through new eyes—a valuable experience. So I have to
thank you as well.'

Both humbled and exhilarated by his words, she felt herself near tears. He moved in the darkness and under her shawl his hand slid up her bare arm to her shoulder while his other hand raised her chin. Deliberately he lowered his mouth to hers.

His kiss began gently, almost tenderly, so that she was disarmed. Her body pliant, she leaned towards him, stroking his cheeks, playing with his hair, exulting in the greater demand of his mouth. Inexperienced and untutored though her response might have been, it was still undoubtedly a response, and in the man it unleashed an urgency, a passion, that quickly seized them both. His hands roamed her body. His lips left her mouth to slide down her neck to her throat, where the pulse was a primitive drumbeat in her blood. She was scarcely aware of him pushing the straps from her shoulders, for he was kissing her again, his mouth a delicious invasion. But then his hand slid under her dress to cup the fullness of her breast. His touch was like fire and he must have felt the shock that rippled through her body, the sudden tension. 'I won't hurt you,' he murmured against her mouth, nibbling at her lips with his teeth so that unconsciously her body trembled like a leaf in the wind. 'You're so beautiful, Shannon, and I want you so much——' He broke off, giving a sudden exclamation.

'What's wrong?' she asked in bewilderment.

'Someone just switched on the outdoor light. And I've just noticed that there's a car parked by the garage—a black Mercedes.'

'My mother—she must have come home early,' Shannon said incoherently, straightening her dress with fingers that shook, so rapid had been the transition from bliss to cold reality.

'You're frightened of her.'

She nodded bleakly. 'It's ridiculous, isn't it? I'm twenty-one years old—but yes, I am frightened of her.'

'I'm coming in with you.'

'You'd better not—I'm sure she'll be cross.'

'All the more reason for me to come then.'

'But, Blaise——'

'Do you remember what I said yesterday? I said you've got to trust me. So trust me now, Shannon. Come along.'

Before she could protest any further, he had pulled her out of the car and she was following him up the steps. The door swung open, and the couple was bathed in light: the tall blond man faultlessly attired in a black tuxedo, his eyes a startling blue, his harshly carved features strong and uncompromising; the graceful girl at his side in her long green dress, her face flushed and vivid, her mouth still soft from his lovemaking.

'So you're finally home, Shannon,' Lorna Hart said in the crisp, well-modulated voice she used when she was angry.

Very conscious of Blaise at her side, Shannon said with attempted lightness, 'Yes, I'm home—and I've had a wonderful evening. Mother, I'd like you to meet——'

'I don't really think introductions will be necessary,' Lorna said briskly. 'You'd better come in and go straight to bed. You know how Dr Snider warned you against getting overtired.'

'I'm not tired,' Shannon retorted. 'I feel fine.'

'I will not tolerate rudeness, Shannon. As I'm the one who has the continued care of you—and having a blind girl on one's hands is not easy—I think you must allow me to be the judge of your health.'

The girl quivered as though she had been struck and visibly her new-found confidence began to seep away. When she had been with Blaise she had almost forgotten she was blind—now she was being forcibly reminded both of her handicap and of its cost to her mother. . . .

Blaise's voice was like a whiplash, and not until then did Shannon realise just how angry he was. 'Mrs Hart,

my name is Blaise Strathern—I'm Rick's half-brother.
I've been out of the country for some months, but on
my return I heard about the accident and I wanted to
find out how your daughter was getting along. I'd like
your permission to take Shannon for a drive tomorrow
afternoon. How about two o'clock again, Shannon?'

Before the girl could reply, Lorna cut in, 'That will
be impossible. Shannon will need to rest tomorrow.'

'Shannon is a very healthy young woman. And it does
her good to get outdoors.'

'Shannon is blind, Mr Strathern,' Lorna said crisply.
'The answer is no. Now, if you'll excuse us, please——'

'Two things, Mrs Hart. First of all, in the future I
shall be encouraging Shannon to become as independent
as possible. And secondly, I shall call for Shannon tomorrow at two. If when I come I'm told I cannot see
her, I shall take the house apart brick by brick until I
find her. I hope that's clear.'

Stunned, Shannon felt his hands drop on her shoulders.
His kiss was brief and hard, his voice reassuringly matter-
of-fact. 'I'll see you tomorrow, Shannon. Thanks again
for a lovely evening.' The door closed behind him.

His words and his touch had somehow given Shannon
the courage she needed. She said calmly, 'You're right,
Mother, I *am* tired. I'd better go straight to bed. I'll
see you in the morning and you can tell me all about
your holiday then. Goodnight.'

Dead silence was the only response. Making her escape, Shannon climbed the stairs and went to her room,
her face thoughtful. Because of Blaise she had been able
to assert herself in a very small way, and probably out
of sheer surprise Lorna had let her get away with it.
But Shannon was under no illusions that the battle was
done . . . tomorrow morning would tell the tale.

Unpinning her hair, she began to brush it out, her
movements slow and reflective. In the last two days a

decision had been made, for she now knew she could not
sink back into the somnolent, dreary half-life she had
been leading since the accident. With Blaise she had
walked on crowded sidewalks, eaten in restaurants,
attended a concert—been among people in the noise and
bustle of the city. Despite her inevitable fears, it had only
whetted her appetite for more; a guide dog at her side
would be the key to even greater freedom. Somehow,
tomorrow morning, she had to convince her mother of
that.

Shannon had just finished breakfast the next morning
when she heard the light fall of her mother's footsteps on
the stairs. She took another sip of coffee, trying to ignore
the frisson of anxiety that ran up and down her spine.
'Good morning,' she said brightly. 'Did you sleep well?'

'As well as could be expected.'

Hardly an encouraging response. Still trying to speak
pleasantly, Shannon said, 'Did you buy some new clothes
in California? What are you wearing now?'

Usually Lorna could be diverted by talk of her wardrobe, but not today. 'A light green pantsuit,' she said
shortly.

Even early in the morning Lorna would be perfectly
groomed, Shannon knew, every hair on her blonde head
in place, her make-up flawless, her long fingernails
shaped and polished. She would be tanned after two
weeks in the sunshine; because she exercised rigorously
her figure would be trim and neat. At forty-nine, Lorna
could have passed for forty; most of her life revolved
around preserving appearances and keeping at bay the
inevitable signs of ageing.

The clink of a spoon against china meant Lorna was
starting the unsweetened grapefruit that together with
black coffee constituted her breakfast. 'Shannon, I hope
you've come back to your senses now that you've had a

good night's sleep. I'm sure Mr Strathern's attentions have been all very flattering, but obviously they can't go on for ever. I don't know what kind of game he's playing, holding out false promises to you, but it has to end.'

Shannon took a deep breath. 'Mother, all he's done is to show me I have a choice—to remain the way I am, or to try and make the very best of a bad situation. It's *my* choice, not his. I want to get out more, to be among people, to go places and do things.' She hesitated, then plunged on. 'We don't often talk of my father, do we, but when I was trying to decide what to do, I couldn't help feeling he would have encouraged me——'

'Your father!' Lorna spat with a violence that seemed totally out of proportion to Shannon. 'I will not have you like your father—here today, gone tomorrow, always flying off to some godforsaken place, never home when I needed him. Your place is with me.'

'Mother, I——'

'You owe it to me,' Lorna swept on. 'It hasn't been easy for me, bringing you up since you were five years old all alone. And even before that your father was precious little help.'

Appalled as much by the venom in Lorna's voice as by this new perspective on her parents' marriage, Shannon said in a small voice, 'Didn't you love him?' Unbidden there came into the girl's mind an image of her handsome father, laughing in the sun, as he tossed his little daughter high in the air and caught her, tickling her until she squealed.

'No—I detested him!'

'Perhaps that's why he didn't want to be home.'

Lorna's cup rattled against the saucer. 'We didn't come here to discuss your father,' she said sharply. 'We're discussing you.'

'You're afraid that I'll turn out like him, aren't you, and go away and leave you alone?' Shannon said gently, for the first time in her life gaining some understanding of her mother's almost pathological possessiveness. 'I won't do that——'

'Stop talking like some kind of psychoanalyst,' Lorna snapped. 'After all the years I've devoted to you, you owe me something. I don't want you seeing this Blaise Strathern again. He's obviously a bad influence on you.'

'How so?' Shannon asked almost absently, her mind still grappling with the implications of what she had heard.

'I can see a change in you—you're rude and assertive——'

'I think you should be congratulating him,' Shannon replied drily. Suddenly desperately sincere, she went on, 'Mother, don't you see? He's brought me to life, he's given me new confidence and pride in myself, new ambition—aren't you glad?' It was a cry from the heart.

'I can only repeat that I do not want him coming here any more—and this afternoon I shall tell him so.'

Shannon leaned forward, her fingers gripping the starched white tablecloth. 'All he wants me to do is learn Braille, and get a guide dog—that's all.'

'There'll be no more talk of these dogs!'

'If I had one, I could go out by myself. I could even go back to university. Mother——'

'You are not having one.'

Calling on all her reserves, Shannon said, 'I'm twenty-one years old—you can't stop me.'

Her mother gave an unpleasant laugh. 'My dear child, you're forgetting one very essential thing—money. You have none of your own. And I shall certainly not give you the money for such a hare-brained scheme.'

Under the table Shannon's knees were shaking. 'Don't you want me to overcome my blindness? You should be delighted that I want to become more independent, less of a burden to you.'

'You're ignoring the facts, child,' Lorna said coldly. 'Suppose you do manage to get your degree—although I don't see how you possibly can—then what? Do you think you'd ever get a job? Of course you wouldn't. The whole idea is ludicrous. Mr Strathern is being very cruel to raise false hopes in you.'

Despite herself, Shannon quailed before the conviction in her mother's voice—was she right? Maybe she was ... maybe it was better to accept her limitations rather than to struggle against them.

As though she sensed her daughter's weakening, Lorna drove the point home. 'This afternoon I shall tell him you don't want to see him again. It will be the best thing for you in the long run, believe me, Shannon.'

Shannon pressed her hands to her face, too confused and upset to reply. Who was right? Blaise with his forcefulness, his insistence that she fight her handicap? Or her mother, telling her to be realistic and accept her lot?

Lorna pushed her chair back decisively. 'I'm having two tables of bridge this evening, so you can come down and chat with people as they arrive. I just hope that Jessie will play better bridge than last time—her calling was atrocious. Now I'd better speak to Bridget about the food. And the living room needs a good cleaning. I think she let things slide while I was away.'

Shannon sat still, knowing that for Lorna the matter was closed. She, Shannon, would stay home this afternoon, and this evening would make pleasant and dutiful conversation with the asthmatic Colonel Fawcett, the heavily gallant Dr Snider, and the fluttery Jessie Harper.

She couldn't stand it, she couldn't. . . . She went to stand by the open window, through which wafted the garden's fragrance, the sounds of cars passing and children calling, a dog barking . . . the world beckoning her, urging her to become part of it. She sank down on the window seat, leaning her forehead against the glass.

CHAPTER FOUR

After lunch Shannon went to her room, ostensibly to rest after her late night; it had already been made clear that Lorna was to deal with Blaise when he came at two o'clock. Shutting the door behind her, Shannon went to the wardrobe and found her jeans and an embroidered blouse, then hastily pulled off her cashmere skirt and sweater, her carefully matched string of pearls. The action seemed symbolic, she thought recklessly, as she thrust bare feet into thonged sandals. Her mother had never approved of jeans . . . nor would she approve of what Shannon was about to do.

She brushed her hair and splashed on some of her most expensive perfume. Then she opened the door again, listening acutely to the hushed silence of the house before stepping out into the hallway and going down the back stairs. There was what seemed like an agonisingly long wait, although it was actually only three minutes, as Bridget concluded her conversation with the butcher. Then the back door shut and Bridget went through the swing door to the front of the house. The coast was clear.

Carefully feeling her way along the kitchen wall to the back door, Shannon pushed it open. The hinges squealed, and she waited with bated breath for someone to come and investigate. But the only sound was the hum of the vacuum cleaner. Cautiously she stepped out into the sunshine. Keeping one hand on the mellow pink bricks, which were warm to the touch, she edged along the back of the house. Her plan was to wait in the shrubbery along the driveway and intercept Blaise before he went up to the house to find only Lorna waiting for him. It seemed important to Shannon to tell him the true reasons why she would be unable to become more independent, rather than allowing him to hear only what Lorna chose to fabricate. In her mind she had tried to prepare herself for his inevitable departure once she had told him her predicament, for there would be nothing more to hold him when he realised how trapped she was; that it should be lack of money that would imprison her in the cushioned luxury of her mother's house seemed the final irony . . . she pushed back these unproductive thoughts, knowing only too well how much time she would have to dwell on them when Blaise had gone. Right now her task was to secrete herself in the woods without either Bridget or Lorna catching a glimpse of her.

Holding a clear mental picture of the grounds in her mind, Shannon left the shelter of the house and stepped along the grassy path beside the raspberry canes, going past the toolshed and the old stone wall where the honeysuckle grew and all summer the tiny hummingbirds hovered, their breasts gleaming like scarlet jewels. Through the gate until against her face she felt the brush of leaves and underfoot the fragile fronds of ferns. Cautiously feeling her way, she went deeper into the woods.

Years ago she had played in these woods, peopling them with fairies and imaginary playmates and strange animals, every tree trunk and hillock and rock known to her, clothed in friendliness. But now it was different. The undergrowth had grown thick and twisted. Branches scratched her face and protruding roots made her trip. However, she persisted, losing all track of time as she fiercely concentrated on her sense of direction, the only guide she had. All too soon she heard through the trees the sound of a car turning off the road on to the drive-

way, and then the approaching whine of its tyres. He
was early . . . after all her efforts she was going to miss
him.

She stumbled down the slope to the ditch, scratching
her arms on the blackberry vines. Her toe caught against
a rock and she pitched forward on the grass. Paralysingly
close there came the screech of brakes, then the slam of
a car door and a man's footsteps.

'Shannon!' Blaise exclaimed hoarsely, sliding his arms
around her body and half lifting her. 'Dear God, I
thought I was going to hit you—are you all right?'

Fighting back a wave of dizziness and nausea, she
mumbled, 'Sorry—I didn't mean to scare you.'

The piercingly blue eyes scanned her paper-white face,
her scratched arms and hands. She could not see the
whiteness about his mouth, but as he gathered her in
his arms, she felt the drumming of his heart and said
again, 'I'm sorry, Blaise, but I thought I was going to
miss you and you'd go up to the house without seeing
me.'

'Something's wrong, isn't it?' She nodded. 'You don't
want me to go to the house?'

'No. Could we go for a short drive instead? I need to
talk to you.'

'Of course. Let me help you in the car.'

Her legs were trembling from delayed reaction, and it
was a relief to sit down. Blaise got in beside her and
reversed in the driveway. 'Sit back and relax,' he said
quietly. 'We'll talk when we get there.'

She did as she was told, tears of weakness pricking at
her eyes. She had known him such a short time, but
already she had come to depend on his strength, his
paradoxical blend of toughness and gentleness. She
would miss him when he left . . . miss him dreadfully.
She closed her eyes, for the first time conscious of the
scratches on her arms and sore spots on her body.

They drove for perhaps half an hour until the narrow country-road they had been following ended in a rutted track. 'A friend of mine owns this farm,' Blaise told her. 'We'll go up into the orchard—it's sheltered from the wind there.' Under the trees he spread a blanket on the grass and gratefully Shannon sank down on it. 'Now,' he went on, 'tell me what's happened since last night.'

Haltingly at first, then more confidently, she described the scene with her mother that morning, including the disclosures about her parents' marriage and Lorna's final ultimatum. 'I always knew my mother was very possessive, but I never thought it would be to the point of keeping me helpless and dependent on her,' she finished, and there was no disguising the hurt in her voice. 'So you see, it's no good. My mother won't pay for the dog and I can't.' She reached over and rested her hand on his arm, her lovely jade eyes fastened on his face. 'But Blaise, even though it hasn't worked out, I do want to thank you for trying. I just wish——' She broke off, her cheeks flushed.

'What do you wish, Shannon?'

'I'll miss you when you're gone,' she said with devastating simplicity.

'So you think this is the end of it?'

Surprised, she said, 'Well, of course.'

His voice was very matter-of-fact. 'There's been a new development—I didn't want to tell you about it yesterday until the details were settled. But first, you do realise you're fighting two separate battles, don't you? There's your blindness, of course. But also you must break free of your mother's domination.'

From higher on the hillside a robin carolled, and from the woods beyond the orchard there came an answering ripple of song. 'It's a lot to ask,' she said in a small voice. 'I'm all my mother has——'

'Nonsense. She's a wealthy woman with a beautiful

house and her own circle of friends. Don't ignore the facts.'

'Don't dramatise, you mean.'

'That, too.'

She would need time to think over what he had said, although once again she sensed he was right. 'What's the new development you mentioned?'

'I want you to listen very carefully, Shannon, and not interrupt until I'm finished,' he ordered, an edge of steel in his voice. 'I spoke to the doctor who looked after you in Vancouver after the accident, and he put me in touch with a Dr MacAuley in Toronto—a relatively young man, but already known as a brilliant eye surgeon. On the basis of your past history he thinks it's worthwhile for you to go to Toronto. You'll be admitted to hospital and he'll do a series of tests and then decide what the chances would be of a successful operation.'

Shannon leaned forward, her hand gripping Blaise's wrist so hard that the fingernails dug into his flesh. 'You mean—I might be able to see again?'

'Dr MacAuley wants you to go to Toronto, Shannon —that's all I'm saying. No promises. No guarantees.'

The wild hope that had flared in her breast shrivelled and died. 'So I could go all the way there for nothing?'

'Yes.'

She suddenly became aware that she was holding him; releasing his wrist, she let her hands fall back in her lap and consciously tried to relax them. Slowly a little colour seeped back into her cheeks. 'No, Blaise, I won't go.'

'Why not?' he rapped.

'I couldn't bear to go all the way there and then have to come straight back.'

'You're assuming the worst.'

'Anyway, I never want to go into a hospital again.'

'I've booked two seats on a direct flight from Victoria to Toronto, leaving tomorrow morning.'

He had spoken so quietly that it took a minute for his words to sink in. Raising her chin, she said flatly, 'Well, you can cancel them.'

'No, Shannon.'

'Blaise, I'm not going. Dr Snider said there was no chance of——'

'Dr Snider is a general practitioner. The specialist in Vancouver encouraged me to send you.'

Again that irrational hope leaped in her heart. 'He did?' she whispered.

Blaise took her by the shoulders, his piercing blue eyes fastened on her delicate features. 'What have you got to lose?' he said forcibly.

'Nothing, I suppose.' There was a sudden bitter twist to her mouth. 'I certainly can't get worse, can I?' Then she added hopelessly, 'But I can't go anyway, Blaise. I haven't any money. And after this afternoon I'm sure my mother won't give me any.'

'The tickets are paid for.'

'I can't allow you to do that!'

'It's already done. And your mother will just have to make the best of it, won't she?'

Everything was moving too fast. 'I—I'm scared, Blaise.'

'Of course you are. It's a big risk, Shannon—but one you have to take.'

'You make everything seem so simple and straightforward.' Wanting to touch him, she rested a hand on his leg. 'I never used to talk to Rick like this,' she confessed. 'I don't know why. . . .'

'The circumstances are very different,' he said harshly. 'After all, you and Rick were in love.'

She could feel the warmth of his thigh against her fingertips. She and Rick had been in love, happy together, so perhaps there had been no need to talk the way she and Blaise did. But if there had been that need

—would she have felt the same trust in Rick's judgment, the same confidence in his strength? It did not seem very likely. . . .

'I wish there was some way I could convince you that Rick isn't worth your little finger.'

Startled by the suppressed violence in his voice, she looked up, wanting to share her doubts with him. But before she could speak, he reached over, roughly pulling her down on the blanket beside him, and his mouth silenced whatever she might have said.

It was as though in one kiss he was trying to erase from her mind all memories of Rick. It was an attack against which she was defenceless, for at the first touch of his lips she knew this was what she wanted, this was what she had been asking for when she had put her hand on his leg. Reassurance from the fears he had raised. Closeness and intimacy. A slow-spreading warmth that exploded into flame as his kiss grew deeper and his body moulded itself to hers. She was beleaguered by a host of new sensations and surrendered herself to them in delight: the softness of her breasts against his chest; the long length of his thigh falling over her legs; the pulsating hardness of his masculinity. She needed no words to tell her she was desired. For the first time in her life she felt the urgency of a man's need and in her blood an answering urgency—to give him all that he asked and in the giving to receive something she had never even known she wanted.

When his hand slid under her blouse to hold her breast, she caressed the hard contours of his chest with its tangled mat of hair, through her fingertips instinctively sensing what pleased him. Then his mouth pushed aside the thin fabric of her blouse, following the curve of her flesh to the tip, and for Shannon everything stilled to an exquisite pleasure that for a moment was sufficient enough in itself. But only for a moment. The ache of sweetness in her blood demanded more, pulsing with rhythms as old as time, yet as new to her as the dawn. Instinctively her hips moved against him as her hands held his head against her body and her lips breathed his name.

She felt the shock run through his body as he froze to stillness. Everything was suddenly very quiet and there was only the warmth of the sun on her back and the distant calling of the birds in her ears.

'Blaise—what is it?' Her hands found his face, feeling the tension in his jawline, the taut line of his mouth. 'Please, what's wrong?'

With an abruptness that terrified her, he pulled free of her so that her hands fell empty on the blanket. 'This is crazy,' he said roughly. 'I had no business kissing you like that.'

'Didn't you—like it?'

He raked his fingers through his hair, his blue eyes bitter. 'Of course I did—you're not that much of an innocent, Shannon.'

'I'm not——'

He interrupted her with savage contempt. 'Look, you were engaged to Rick, so don't act as though you've never been kissed before. Knowing Rick as I do, I'm sure you're not the innocent young virgin you're pretending to be.'

In one swift movement she sat up, her blouse still disarrayed, exposing the creamy skin of her throat and breast. There were bright patches of colour in her cheeks and her hair glowed like polished wood in the sun. 'As it happens, you're wrong, Blaise Strathern! I never made love to Rick.'

'Shannon, he told me that you did.'

She rocked backwards, her face blank with shock. 'Then he was lying,' she said.

'Why would he bother lying about a thing like that?'

Why indeed? She banged her fist on her knee in utter

frustration. 'I have no idea,' she retorted. 'All I can tell you is the truth—I never made love with Rick. Or with anyone else, for that matter.'

Blaise said heavily, 'Be that as it may——'

'You don't believe me, do you? You don't believe one word I've said!'

'I don't want to discuss it any more, Shannon,' he said sharply. 'What you and Rick did—or didn't do—is your business. But I'm the one who started making love to you today—and for that I apologise. Under the circumstances it was the last thing I should have done.'

Her voice was very quiet, her body braced against whatever might come. 'Under the circumstances?' Only silence answered her question and she knew he was at a loss to reply. 'Let me answer for you,' she said with deadly precision. 'Because I'm blind—that's what you were going to say, isn't it?'

Again a pause. 'That's only part of it, Shannon, and it's not the way you think. Right now I can't explain it to you.'

But she was no longer listening. Aimlessly her fingers plucked at the blades of grass, shredding them to pieces. 'Please will you take me home?'

'Yes.' A pause. 'Shannon?'

She looked up in sudden hope, but all he said was, 'Whatever happens, I want you to remember I'm on your side.'

Bewildered, obscurely frightened, she no longer knew what to believe. 'Are you? Are you really, Blaise?'

A hand took her arm. As she recoiled, his grip dropped immediately. 'Yes—that I do promise.'

Her voice was only a ragged whisper. 'I want to go home.'

Although home, she thought wearily, would only be another battle, this time with her mother. It was a battle she had expected to fight alone, but when they pulled up in front of the house, Blaise said flatly, 'I'm coming in with you.'

It was Bridget who opened the door. 'Oh, Shannon dearie, I was so worried! And your mother—she's been beside herself,' she added in a stage whisper that at any other time might have been amusing.

'Where is Mrs Hart?' Blaise asked coolly.

'I'm here, Mr Strathern. You look a fright, Shannon. What on earth have you been doing—trying to elope?'

Shannon flinched, but before she could reply, Blaise said grimly, 'You're about as far from the truth as you could imagine. Tomorrow I'm taking Shannon to Toronto to see an eye specialist—there's the possibility of an operation.'

'That's out of the question!'

'I think you will find that your daughter has made up her own mind.'

'That's neither here nor there,' Mrs Hart snapped, and Shannon could imagine only too well the glaze of anger in her pale blue eyes. 'I've already made it clear to Shannon that I am not prepared to pay for any of your ridiculous schemes.'

'And I've made it clear that I shall finance her.'

Shannon waited tensely, knowing that for once Lorna had met her match. 'I see,' the older woman said with deceptive mildness. 'And what are you getting in return, Mr Strathern?'

'Mother!' the girl exclaimed, pressing hands to her hot cheeks. 'It's not like that—he only wants to help me.'

Lorna laughed cruelly. 'You do have a lot to learn, Shannon. Your naïvety is charming, but just a little out of place.'

There was a note in Blaise's voice that Shannon had never heard before. 'I will not tolerate your insinuations, Mrs Hart. I feel a sense of responsibility towards Shannon because of what Rick did—and that's all.'

Was he telling the truth? Shannon wondered, her heart sinking in her breast. If so, what about those kisses on the hillside—what had they meant? Perhaps her mother was right and she was far too naïve—perhaps Blaise had been wanting something in return for his money. In sudden revulsion she said coldly, 'Mr Strathern is quite right, Mother. It's purely a business arrangement. And no matter who pays, I'm determined to go.'

'I thoroughly dislike your defiant attitude,' her mother replied sharply.

'I'm sorry—but what I'm fighting for is desperately important to me.'

'I see,' her mother replied. 'Well, if you're determined on this course, Shannon, I certainly will not have it bandied about the neighbourhood that I can't afford my daughter's upkeep—so I shall pay all the expenses. Your money will not be necessary, Mr Strathern.'

'Very good,' he said, and from his tone of voice Shannon could gain no clue as to his emotions. 'I'll pick you up tomorrow morning around eight-thirty, Shannon. The flight leaves at ten, and I'm to book you into the hospital as soon as we get to Toronto.'

'Thank you, she said, repelled by his impersonal manner and certain that in front of her mother he would not touch her. Nor did he.

'Goodnight, Mrs Hart,' he said formally. 'And Shannon—remember that promise I made.'

Her mind a jumble of conflicting emotions, Shannon heard the door close behind him. For one crazy moment she wanted to run after him, begging him to take her with him, longing to feel his arms come hard around her and his mouth imprint itself on hers. Terrified that these thoughts might be showing on her face, she turned to face her mother, bracing herself for whatever might come.

'What are the chances of success of this operation?'

'I don't know. The doctor may even decide not to do one,' Shannon said miserably.

'The whole thing is ridiculous,' Lorna snapped. 'As I said once before, this man seems intent upon raising your hopes for nothing. But it's obvious you're not listening to a word I say any more.'

In her heart Shannon was afraid her mother might be right about Blaise. Stubbornly she said, 'I have to try. Would you mind asking Bridget to come and help me pack, please?' With the feeling that she had won at least a small victory, she began to climb the stairs.

Just over twenty-four hours later the nurse, whom Shannon pictured as short and pretty, said brightly, 'Do you have everything you need now, Miss Hart?'

She had been exceptionally friendly, easing the situation for Shannon, who had found the re-entrance into the hospital world a frightening experience: it had raised too many old memories that she would have preferred to forget. So now she said, 'Please—call me Shannon.'

'And I'm Anita,' the little nurse replied promptly. 'I'll be on this shift for the next two weeks, so we'll be seeing a lot of each other. And I might as well tell you you're in the care of the best doctor in this hospital—if anything can be done, Dr MacAuley will do it. If you need anything, press this little buzzer. Visiting hours are over at nine, and I'll come back then and get you settled for the night. I'm sure you'll sleep well—you've had a long day.'

It had been a long day, Shannon thought. The chill goodbyes from her mother offset by Bridget's tearful hug; the long plane journey across the mountains and prairies and Great Lakes; the confusion of Toronto airport and the downtown traffic; the inevitable red tape for admission to the hospital. But all day Blaise had been at her side, his arm steadying her and his voice guiding her.

She could not have done it alone, she knew.

The nurse bustled out, and from the corridor Shannon heard her speak to Blaise. The girl leaned back on the pillow. Bridget had purposely packed her prettiest negligee with creamy lace edging; her hair was brushed smooth to frame her face, that was grave and shadowed with weariness. Yet her beauty, unadorned by make-up, made its own statement against the white pillows.

She heard Blaise come into the room, and smiled. 'Hello.'

He had halted at the foot of the bed, and there was a tiny silence. Then, 'You look very lovely,' he said, a strange note in his voice.

She blushed and for the hundredth time wished she could see him. Were his sky-blue eyes smiling at her? Was the light caught in the thick blond hair? Shyly she patted the bed. 'Come and sit down.'

Again that fractional hesitation before she felt his weight settle on the mattress. 'I brought you some flowers.'

She took the cellophane-wrapped bouquet, superstitiously aware of an uncanny sense of repetition: a year ago in a hospital many miles away, Rick had given her flowers. 'What are they?' she asked, her voice suddenly anxious.

She felt his hands undo the wrapping. 'Red roses,' he said quietly. 'Because of your courage and because of the promise I made you.'

'Oh. . . .' Not knowing what to say, she buried her face in the fragrant, dusky petals. Red roses were for love, she knew that as well as must he, and the thought brought a tinge of red to her cheeks and a wayward excitement to her breast. But he was speaking again. . . .

'When this is all over, Shannon, I've arranged for you to spend a couple of weeks at my father's summer place in the Gatineau hills. After the operation, you won't be able to fly for a while, and this will give you the chance to recuperate.'

'You seem very sure I'll have an operation,' she said, her throat tightening with panic.

'I guess I am.' Another long pause.

She frowned slightly. 'Blaise, is anything wrong? You're very quiet.'

He said abruptly, 'There's something I have to tell you.'

Ridiculous that the panic should transform itself to sheer terror. 'Oh? What's that?'

'I'm leaving Toronto tonight, Shannon. I'll be away for at least a week.'

She felt as though she had been slapped, for in two short sentences he had whisked her only security away from her. Ice-cold, her voice sounding very far away, she stumbled, 'You mean you won't be here while he's doing the tests—and then maybe the operation?'

He took her hands between his, where they lay, limp and unresponsive. Chafing them gently to give them warmth he said, 'I'm sorry, Shannon, more sorry than I can say——'

'I'd counted on you being here.' Her hair falling forward to hide her face, she blurted without any finesse, 'I need you.'

For a moment his fingers tightened so cruelly on hers that she gasped with pain. 'Sorry,' he muttered. 'Look, Shannon, let me explain. I told you I was an archaeologist, didn't I? There's a dig up north investigating a possible landing site of the Vikings and the man who was to have headed it up just had a serious heart attack. So they phoned me last night to see if I'd go up there in his place. There's a lot of preparation and money tied up in this expedition, and in terms of potential findings it's a very significant one—they need me to at least get things underway.'

She had listened numbly to this explanation, but one phrase had leaped out at her. 'You knew about this since last night?'

'Yes.'

'Why didn't you tell me before this?' she demanded, snatching her fingers away from his. 'I thought you'd be here the whole time.'

'I know you did.' She could not see the implacable glint in his eye, but it was there in his intonation for her to hear. 'I purposely didn't tell you, Shannon, because I was afraid if I did that you wouldn't come here.'

'You deliberately deceived me,' she whispered, appalled.

He shifted on the bed and she could feel his breath warm on her cheek. She shrank back against the pillows. 'I had to, Shannon, don't you see? I had no choice.'

'And yet you tell me to trust you?'

His hands were gripping her shoulders now, almost shaking her. 'Just answer me one question,' he grated. 'If I'd told you this last night—would you have come today?'

Struggling to be free of his hold, she said wildly, 'I don't know—how can I know that?'

'I don't think you would have,' he said heavily. 'And I wasn't prepared to risk that. At least you're here now, Shannon, and Dr MacAuley will see you.'

'I don't have to stay,' she cried. 'I'll leave and——'

'How?'

This one little word stopped her. Her body went limp in his grip. With all the bitterness of a year of dependence in her voice, she flailed, 'You've covered all the angles, haven't you? You know I can't leave without you. So I'm trapped here.'

'It will work out for the best, Shannon. Even at the very worst, if the operation's not feasible, you're at least free enough of your mother to be able to go home and go back to university.'

Home . . . it seemed a million miles away. At the thought of the next few days an overwhelming wave of loneliness and fear swept over her, leaving her weak and trembling, and in her heart of hearts she knew Blaise to be right: had she known he would not be there, she would not have come; unconsciously she had been counting on his strength and support to see her through what had to be an ordeal. Now that that support had been withdrawn, she was terrified to realise how much she had come to depend on him—too much, she thought painfully. Hardly recognising her own voice, she heard herself say, 'You Stratherns are all alike, aren't you? First Rick, now you——'

'Stop it, Shannon! You know there's no comparison——'

'Oh, I'm forgetting, aren't I? You don't like to be compared to Rick.' She could feel the hard sobs rising in her throat and knew she had to get rid of him before, humiliatingly, they broke to the surface. Turning her face away, she gulped, 'Please go now, Blaise—I'm tired, and I've had enough of this.'

'I'm sorry I've upset you, Shannon,' he said grimly. 'But you know, I'd do the same thing again. . . . I'll be thinking of you, and I'll be back as soon as I can. I promise it will be within a week.'

She bit her lip, longing for him to be gone, yet equally longing for his arms to come around her and hold her, shielding her from the dark of the night.

Lips brushed her cheek with the cool impersonality of a stranger's. He got up from the bed and she heard his indrawn breath as though he was about to say something else. She waited, her heartbeat loud in her ears, but there was only the swivel of his heels on the floor and and then the retreat of his steps. The door swung shut behind him.

Shannon shoved her hand against her mouth to prevent herself from crying his name out loud, begging him to come back. The room was quiet and empty, and as she twisted on her stomach, burying her face in the pillow, she caught the elusive scent of roses.

CHAPTER FIVE

AFTERWARDS, when she looked back, the three weeks Shannon spent in hospital could be recalled as a series of sharp images separated by spaces of time that seemed to drag interminably. There was Dr MacAuley's soft Scottish burr asking question after question, his sure, gentle surgeon's hands, and his predilection for atrocious puns that in the tensest moments could always make Shannon laugh. A seventy-five per cent chance of success, he said, and without even thinking Shannon agreed to the operation. There was the blanking out of time by the anaesthetic and then by pain-killing drugs, and then the waiting in the dark, her eyes again covered by bandages, her body striving for the calm and relaxation that was a necessary part of the cure. There was the genuine friendliness and interest of her nurses, all of whom by now had personalities to go with their voices. And through it all ran the aching sense that despite the doctor and the nurses, despite a stiffly worded and quite unexpected telegram from her mother, she was alone.

Blaise had said he would think of her, but she had no sense of him reaching out to her across the thousand miles that separated them. He had said he would be back in a week, but seven days passed, then eight, nine, ten, and still there was no sign of him, no word from him. Inevitably Shannon began to wonder, during the long hours that she lay flat on her back in the dimmed room, if he had not deceived her in more than simply his trip up north. His promise that he was on her side—what did it mean in the light of this total abandonment? His care and tact that had given her the courage to go out in public, his private insistence that she jerk herself out of the passive life-style that had been smothering her —had they all been a façade, a game to him?

During the first week in hospital she missed him and would catch herself listening for the familiar fall of his footsteps, hoping to hear the deep, confident timbre of his voice. But as the days slowly passed and he did not come, hurt and disillusion overcame this hope, and resentment began to build. She had thought him different from Rick—but he was the same. And in both cases for her the end result was the same—she had been left alone at a time when she was in need. Almost she began to dread Blaise's return. She did not want to hear his explanations and excuses, his voice saying things that she no longer would be able to believe.

Then, finally, came the day when the bandages were removed and for Shannon there was the miracle of sight restored; she had never seen anything more beautiful in her life than the dim outlines of that hospital room with its pale green walls and utilitarian bureau, its plain white sink and metal cupboards. Don't get too excited now, Dr MacAuley said, but from his voice and the first sight of his bearded, beaming smile, she knew he was delighted by his success. For Shannon it was pure joy, too deep and personal to be put into words, but perhaps the clasp of her fingers on the doctor's arm told him all he needed to know.

More days of lying still, resting, allowing her body to recover from the surgery; still no visitors permitted, and still nothing but silence from Blaise. Somehow she had cherished the thought that he would be there when she was able to see again, and that his would be among the first faces that she would see . . . a foolish longing, for which she chastised herself. Apparently in bringing her to Toronto he had fulfilled his sense of obligation. No more responsibility. No more necessity to see her. For him an episode was over and done with—there was no other conclusion to which she could come. All she wished was that it would not hurt so much, that she would not feel quite so betrayed. . . .

Anita, the nurse on the evening shift, who had turned out to be as pretty as Shannon had imagined her, had assured Shannon that all the arrangements had been made for her trip to the Gatineau hills. 'A chauffeured car is to pick you up this afternoon,' she said, obviously impressed by this.

For Shannon it was frightening rather than impressive, for unless Blaise came with the car, she would be thrown into a world of strangers; because she and Rick had been together on the west coast, Shannon had never met his parents. To give herself courage she dressed very carefully in the suit she had worn with Blaise what seemed like an age ago; she made up her face and brushed her hair until it shone. Then, because she was early, she turned on the radio to a programme of pre-recorded music and went to stand by the window, gazing down into the street with its constant movement and ever-changing patterns of colour and light and shadow. She did not hear the approaching footsteps. All she heard was a deep voice sounding fractionally—and unusually—uncertain, yet still familiar. 'Hello, Shannon.'

She turned, knowing instantly that all her resentment had vanished in simple pleasure because he was back. Her face was lit up by a wide smile. But slowly the smile faded, for she had not pictured Blaise to look like this: his face would surely be more angular, more strongly masculine; his hair thicker, his eyes a more brilliant blue

. . . then the truth hit her with a sickening jolt. This was not Blaise. This was Rick.

She grasped the window sill for support and he quickly walked forward, his light blue eyes all concern. 'Are you all right? I'm sorry, I didn't mean to startle you.'

'Yes . . . yes, I'm fine. I—I was just surprised to see you, that's all.'

Squarely he met her gaze. 'I'm sure you were,' he said quietly. 'I want to tell you about that on the drive home. Are you ready to go? Blakeney's outside with the car, and I think he's illegally parked, so we'd better hurry.'

She indicated her suitcase and picked up her raincoat; she had already completed all the formalities of signing herself out of the hospital, and said her goodbyes to Dr MacAuley and the nurses. Now, feeling as though she was in a strange kind of emotional limbo, she preceded Rick out of the room wherein she had spent so many long, lonely hours. And as she went she tried not to think of how happy she had been when she had thought Blaise had returned—and how disappointed at her mistake.

They went down the stairs, through the immaculate foyer and the big glass doors into the sunshine of early summer. Shannon put on the very becoming dark glasses that Dr MacAuley had given her, amidst all her confusion deeply grateful for every little detail that caught her eye: the wide boulevard with its fast-moving cars, the leafy trees and the vividly stocked flowerbeds, the blue sky—as blue as Blaise's eyes? She sighed in quick impatience. She must stop thinking about him. It served no purpose, for he had vanished from her life as precipitately as he had arrived. And besides, she was with Rick again, whom a year ago she had loved. . . .

The chauffeur was standing by a luxurious, highly polished black limousine, waiting to take her suitcase from Rick. He touched his peaked hat with one hand in a gesture that was somehow not at all servile. 'Afternoon, ma'am.'

He was tall and very broad-shouldered, with tight black curls under his hat, his broken nose giving a touch of irregularity to an otherwise youthful face. Shannon frowned. 'You look familiar,' she said, aware as she spoke of Rick's impatience; Rick, she remembered, never treated servants as people.

He grinned, his teeth very white; there was a chip off one of the front ones. 'I wondered if you'd remember me, Miss Hart. Sam Blakeney, University of Victoria football team. Pre-law.'

She smiled and held out her hand. 'Of course I remember you—and it's Shannon, please.' She had never known him well, for her mother had not encouraged any participation in extra-curricular activities; he had, she recalled, been engaged to one of the cheerleaders, Lisa DeWitt, a devastatingly attractive blonde with one of the highest I.Q.s on campus.

As though he had read her thoughts, Sam said, 'Lisa's working in Ottawa. So I'd been looking for a summer job as near to Ottawa as I could get and was lucky enough to find this one.' He hesitated. 'I'm really glad your operation worked out.'

'Thanks, Sam——'

'Shannon, we'd better get going,' Rick interrupted impatiently. 'It's a long drive and they'll be waiting dinner for us.'

But Shannon was no longer the biddable young girl she had been a year ago. Coolly, taking her time, she said, 'Nice to see you again, Sam. Let's get together once I'm settled in and you can tell me all the latest campus gossip.'

'Sure—I'd like that.' He held open the back door of the limousine and helped her in.

She and Rick occupied the back while Sam took the

driver's seat, separated from them by sliding panels of glass. With the smoothness that bespoke money, the car moved out into the street.

'It'll be a three or four-hour drive,' Rick said with an assumed calmness that did not deceive Shannon in the least, for she knew he was still irritated by what she had done. 'Do you want to rest?'

'No, not yet.' In an effort to make conversation—yet why should it be an effort?—she said banally, 'It's nice to be out of hospital.'

'I suppose so.'

A silence. Refusing to be intimidated, she went on, 'What are your parents like, Rick? I've never met either of them, remember?'

'Oh, Dad's an ex-Cabinet minister, member of the Senate, honorary president of a couple of companies. He's not often at Hardwoods—too busy. Mother paints and reads and visits back and forth with the neighbours —she's very delicate and has to watch her health. I'm sure you'll like them.'

'It's very kind of them to have me.'

There was a tinge of malice when he spoke. 'It was Blaise's idea, I believe.'

Trying to speak naturally, Shannon asked, 'Is he there?'

'Who, Blaise? No—he's still up north as far as I know. Mucking about in old graves and getting excited about a few broken bits of pottery.'

There was no mistaking the malice now. 'Why don't you like him?' she asked directly.

'You've met him, haven't you?'

Absurdly she felt the urge to defend Blaise. 'That's not answer enough, Rick.'

Almost sulkily Rick said, 'Oh, he's always so sure of himself and so damned overbearing. Don't tell me you liked him?'

'If it hadn't been for him,' she said clearly, 'I'd still be sitting day after day in my mother's living room, blind, dependent, bored and utterly useless. I wouldn't have come for this operation if he hadn't brought me. So I owe him a debt of gratitude I can never repay.'

'Oh, gratitude,' Rick said irritably. 'He was always good at arranging other people's lives for them. Still,' he added, in a transparent effort at a minimal kind of fairness, 'I'm sure he's glad you got your sight back, isn't he?'

She was unable to totally disguise the mortification in her voice. 'I don't expect he knows. He went north before the operation and I haven't heard from him since.'

'That's typical of Blaise's behaviour—when he gets on the trail of someone who lived a thousand years ago, he's completely unreliable. The twentieth century doesn't even exist for him.'

Rick was only confirming something she had already guessed, but nevertheless his words still had the power to hurt; after all Blaise's efforts on her behalf, all his assurances that he cared what happened to her, it seemed incredible that he could forget about her so easily.

Rick had been eyeing her shrewdly. 'That bothers you, doesn't it?'

'I suppose it does,' she said slowly, unwilling to share with anyone just how much it did. In an effort to distract herself she looked at him dispassionately, trying to see what changes the year had wrought in him. His clothing was just as immaculate and expensive as it had always been, his light fair hair as sleek and silky, his face still unlined. There was only the faintest flicker of his eyelids to show that he minded her scrutiny; his pale eyes held hers with only a shadow of unease. On the spur of the moment she decided to bring things into the open. 'It would seem neither of the Strathern brothers is to be depended on in a crisis,' she said with deliberate provocation.

He winced. 'You remember I said to you in the hospital that I needed to talk to you?' he said earnestly. 'You see, I can tell you the truth now, Shannon—up until now, I never could.'

'The truth about what?'

'About why I had to leave you a year ago, break our engagement.'

She was aware of a growing, cold anger. 'You told me why at the time—you'd been promoted and transferred, and a blind wife didn't fit your plans.'

He leaned forward, one arm across the back of the seat; it was an effort for her to remain still, her hands loosely clasped in her lap. 'That was what I told you, yes,' he said, and incongruously Shannon wondered how she could ever have confused his voice with Blaise's—it lacked the depth, the ring of confidence of his half-brother's. 'That was what I *had* to tell you.' He paused impressively.

'I don't know what you mean, Rick,' she replied, apparently unmoved, and again she saw that uneasy flicker of his lids.

'Let me be completely honest, then—although I'm afraid it may hurt you, Shannon. . . .'

She had no idea what he was going to say, and in spite of herself, she felt her nerves tighten in anticipation. But all she said was, 'I'm tougher than I used to be.'

He grinned suddenly with all the flashing charm that she had once loved; her heart twisted painfully. 'I've noticed that.' His voice had a caressing quality that also she could remember all too well. 'You've grown up, haven't you, Shannon? You're even more beautiful than I remember you.'

In sudden panic she said tightly, 'But we're not discussing my beauty or my maturity, are we?'

If he was disconcerted, he managed not to show it this time. 'Very well,' he said deliberately. 'While you were in hospital, and after the doctors had given the verdict on your blindness, your mother came to see me. She told me she wanted the engagement ended.'

Shannon's jaw dropped. Whatever she had expected, it had not been this. 'But why?' she demanded.

He took her hands in his, although she scarcely noticed. 'Let's get one thing straight first, Shannon—I loved you and I wanted you for my wife. Of course I felt terrible that you were blind—but that didn't change matters for me at all. I still wanted to marry you. Do you believe me?' Helplessly she shrugged her shoulders, her eyes pleading with him to go on. 'But your mother forced me to see things in a different light. You would need constant care, she said. You couldn't be left alone. You couldn't go out by yourself. You certainly couldn't be the hostess at a dinner party, or the guest at a cocktail party. Even the question of children—how could you have looked after a baby? She made me understand that our marriage would have placed an intolerable burden on you, one you couldn't possibly have coped with.'

Shannon sat very still, knowing only too well that her mother could indeed have said every word he had just repeated. 'And you believed her?'

'What choice did I have? She felt that the only place for you was your own home—it was familiar ground and Bridget would be able to help look after you.' He hesitated. 'I don't think it was an easy decision for your mother, because she could easily have encouraged our marriage and that would have removed the problem. But she was convinced that the home environment and a mother's care were what you needed, and she was willing to sacrifice some of her own independence for that. I've never admired your mother more than I did that day.'

He brought out a gold cigarette case and lighter and lit a cigarette. 'Once I realised how much better off you'd be at home, I knew I'd have to break our engagement—and that was the hardest thing I ever did in my life, Shannon. The promotion had been in the offing for some time, but the opening in Quebec was pure chance. I took it—and used that as the reason for breaking our engagement. I couldn't tell you the truth.' For the first time he looked away from her, gazing out of the window; she had always admired the classic lines of his profile. When he finally turned back to her, he said simply, 'I had your own good at heart, Shannon, and that's all I can say—except to ask if you can possibly forgive me.'

Her mind was whirling with the implications of all that he had said. In view of Lorna's behaviour when Blaise had appeared on the scene, Rick's story was only too plausible; Lorna could well have manipulated the breaking of her daughter's engagement. For the first time it occurred to Shannon to wonder why she had allowed it in the first place. . . .

'At least say you believe me, Shannon.'

He had taken her hands again. 'I—I suppose I have to, don't I? But you must give me time to think about it, Rick—it's been a shock to me. Seeing you again, first of all, and then hearing this story.'

Because she was staring at their linked hands, she missed the flash of calculation in his pale eyes. 'Of course, honey,' he said smoothly. 'As soon as I heard you were coming to Hardwoods, I arranged my work schedule so we could spend as much time together as possible. But I did want to clear up the matter of our engagement right away—it was very important to me to finally tell you the truth.'

She gazed at him in perplexity, unable to be anything but impressed by his sincerity and straightforwardness. 'Thank you, Rick, I understand that.' Briefly her hand squeezed his before she withdrew it. 'Do you mind if I try and sleep for a while now? I still get very tired, and Dr MacAuley warned me against overdoing it.'

'Of course not,' he said soothingly. 'The seat will tilt back, and there's a pillow in the back here. Make yourself comfortable.'

Shannon leaned back, closing her eyes with an unconscious sigh of relief and deliberately emptying her mind of all that Rick had told her. Lulled by the motion of the car, she drifted off to sleep.

Some time later Rick's hand gently shaking her arm awoke her. 'We're nearly there, Shannon. Another ten minutes.'

She blinked, trying to drive the cobwebs from her brain. 'Already?' she mumbled.

He laughed indulgently. 'You've been asleep for nearly three hours.'

Shannon reached for her handbag, and hurriedly ran a comb through her hair and repaired her make-up. Only then did she look around her. The city had long been left behind, and the car was following a paved secondary road that wound in a leisurely fashion through rolling hills, newly clad in the fresh greens of early summer. On the right a river meandered alongside them, the late afternoon sun gleaming gold in its sheltered pools. Cattle grazed in the pastures; in the next field a tractor was ploughing tidy rows of parallel lines into the rich soil. The occasional house with its accompanying barns all seemed uniformly well kept, nor was this impression of pastoral neatness dispelled as they turned up a narrow lane that led between a double row of carefully spaced elm trees. Shannon had heard before the comparison of well tended lawns to velvet and had privately scoffed at it; but these lawns, clipped and manicured, were the soft unvarying green of a sweep of fabric. There were evergreens shaped into cones, hedges clipped to rectangles, square flowerbeds and a circular lily pond; and dominating them all, three stories high, a white Colonial-style house with enough columns and shutters and small-paned windows to satisfy any architect. Faintly amused, Shannon wondered how the owner of all this—who was unquestionably a very rich man—could bear to have anyone living here; a human being, she felt, would disturb the estate's exquisite symmetry.

Rick, obviously, saw nothing amiss. As he helped her out of the car, he said with complete satisfaction, 'All this will be mine one day—it was my mother's originally. Let's go in and meet them. There's half an hour before dinner. Dad insists on regular hours—so we can relax with a drink. Sam will look after your case.'

Turning her head, Shannon mischievously winked at Sam, who soberly winked back. Somewhat heartened, she meekly followed Rick up to the front door, which was complete with brass knocker and bell, brass lanterns, and a fanlight. Rick ushered her in, leading her through the high-ceilinged entrance hall down a panelled passageway to the living room.

Again Shannon was conscious of that touch of amusement: the room reeked equally of modernity and money, but she herself could not have lived with its tubular chairs, glass-topped tables, and abstract paintings as obsessively geometrical as the garden outside the tall plate glass windows. At first she thought the room was empty apart from a statue-like Burmese cat and a forest of indoor plants, but then, from behind a carved Oriental screen, a voice said petulantly, 'Charles, get me another drink, please. I can't imagine where Stepton's got to.'

'It's Rick, Mother. I've brought Shannon to meet you.'

The voice warmed to life. 'So you're back, darling—marvellous! Come and see me—I've had a perfectly exhausting day and I just had to lie down.'

Louise Strathern was probably about the same age as

Lorna Hart, but there the resemblance ended. Louise
had a great mass of suspiciously black hair intricately
coiled on her head, calling attention to an excellent
profile very like her son's, while under long curved lids
her eyes were a slumbrous grey. Her full lips were
coloured a shade of carmine that many a younger woman
might have hesitated to use. Stretched out gracefully on
a brocade-covered sofa, she was wearing an intricately
draped tea-gown of pastel chiffon with emeralds gleaming against her still-beautiful skin. She was as sleek and
complacent as a cat, Shannon thought.

Rick made the introductions and Shannon was offered
a languid, scarlet-nailed hand to shake. 'So pleased you're
here, my dear,' Louise murmured. 'I hope you'll have a
pleasant stay.'

'Thank you. It's very kind of you to have me, Mrs
Strathern.'

'No trouble, my dear.'

Very little would trouble Louise Strathern, Shannon
thought ironically, already realising that if anything in-
convenient were to occur, Louise would simply drift
away until it was all over. But Louise's next words wiped
the smile from her eyes. 'You're Blaise's friend, aren't
you?'

'Well—yes. It was he who——'

'I thought so.' Undoubted satisfaction in the mellow
voice.

Rick said sharply, 'A year ago Shannon was engaged
to me, Mother.'

'Oh yes, you were engaged, weren't you?' said Louise
vaguely, examining the perfect oval of one fingernail.
'You look very young, Shannon, I'm sure it was a wise
decision to call it off.'

At Rick's look of bafflement, Shannon had to choke
back a laugh. Then, knowing nothing but a direct question would get her anywhere, she said bluntly, 'Have you

heard from Blaise, Mrs Strathern?'

'Please, dear, call me Louise. Mrs Strathern does sound rather stuffy, don't you think? Blaise? Why would I have heard from Blaise?'

'Well, wasn't he supposed to be coming back here when he finished up north?'

'Perhaps . . . I really don't remember. I gave up trying to keep track of Blaise years ago. Rick darling,' and indefinably her voice took on life, 'do get me another drink. You know how to mix them just as I like them. And perhaps Blaise's little friend would like something too.'

Obediently Rick got up, leaving Shannon to cope with a mixture of amusement that the woman could so blatantly have warned her off Rick, and pure rage at the casual way Blaise had been dismissed. She said clearly, 'Blaise told me he would only be gone a week, and now it's nearly a month. Aren't you worried that something might have happened to him?'

A faint puckering of the beautiful brows. 'Heavens, no. Blaise is well able to look after himself.' Louise shuddered artistically. 'He leads a dreadful life, my dear, always out in the wilds trying to dig up things that in my opinion are better left buried.'

'Do you have an address or a phone number where he could be reached?' Shannon persisted.

'I think he went to Newfoundland—or was that last time?' In relief Louise smiled at the newcomer who had just entered. 'Oh, here's Charles—ask him.'

Shannon already knew that Charles Strathern was the father of both Blaise and Rick, his first wife having been Blaise's mother. Now, as he walked towards her with his hand outstretched, she saw with a pang a pair of sky-blue eyes, very different from Rick's. Blaise's eyes. . . . 'What did you want to ask me, young lady?' he said genially.

Although at sixty Charles Strathern was silver-haired with a rather florid complexion, he was still broad-shouldered and very upright; what Bridget would have called a 'fine figure of a man'. He had all the ease and confidence of one long associated with politics, yet Shannon could not help noticing that the practised smile did not quite reach his eyes. Outwardly composed, she said, 'I was just wondering if you knew how I could get in touch with Blaise?'

She was right: the smile had not reached those eyes; at the mention of his elder son's name a shutter dropped over them and they became completely opaque. It made a disturbing contrast to the bluff voice. 'I'm afraid there are no telephones where he is. Now, can I get you a drink, Miss Hart? Or may I call you Shannon?' He consulted his watch. 'Yes, fourteen minutes until dinner is served, so there's time enough.'

It was clear that the subject of Blaise was closed. Conscious of the beginnings of a headache, Shannon sipped a very mild gin and tonic as she submitted with as good grace as possible to Charles Strathern's catechism on her family and upbringing. The dinner, all five courses of it, was both delicious and interminable, and by the end of it the headache had become a reality. As they got up from the table Rick said quietly, 'You look tired, Shannon. Do you want to go to your room?'

She smiled at him gratefully, for it was not like him to be overly perceptive. 'Yes, I would, please. If you'll excuse me, Louise?'

'Certainly, my dear. I never get up before noon, but I'm sure you can amuse yourself in the morning. Stepton will show you up.'

'That's all right, Mother, I'll show Shannon the way,' Rick said casually.

There was a flicker of something far from sleepy in the grey eyes, and Shannon said uncomfortably, 'I can find my room, I'm sure, Rick.'

'Where is she, Mother?'

'I put her in the east wing as Blaise is away, dear.'

As Shannon and Rick left the room, Rick said ruefully, 'My room's in the west wing, naturally—trust Mother!' He slipped a hand under her elbow as they climbed the elegant, curved staircase, and Shannon was glad of his support, for she was suddenly desperately weary. Too many new impressions in too short a time—that, and a tiny nibbling of unease whenever she thought of Blaise. As though he had read her mind, Rick remarked, 'I thought you rather overdid your concern for Blaise— sooner or later Mother is going to have to realise you're my friend again, not his.'

They were walking down a wide carpeted hallway and Rick pushed open a door. Shannon said evenly, 'Can't I be both?'

He halted with his hand on the doorknob and for a moment there was the same feral glint in his eyes as she had seen in Louise's. 'No, you can't!'

'Why not?'

'Blaise and I have never shared anything yet.'

'Perhaps it's time you started.'

'Not with you, Shannon.'

Neither of them had raised their voices above the normal level, yet somehow Shannon felt as though they had been screaming at each other. 'This doesn't seem to be getting us anywhere, does it?' she said. 'I'll see you tomorrow—what time do you get home from work?'

'I have a meeting at one-thirty . . . say four o'clock.'

She smiled wanly, 'Well, thank you for everything you've done today. Goodnight, Rick.'

He ran his hands up her arms to her shoulders. Because of the door she could not move back, and besides, it seemed undignified to struggle. He lowered his face to hers and although she tried to turn her cheek, he found her mouth. It was a kiss more passionate than she was used to from Rick; and it left her totally unmoved. When he stepped back his light blue eyes were watchful, anger in their depths. 'You're very tired,' he said. 'But we'll improve on that next time. Goodnight, Shannon.'

It was utter relief to be left alone. Scarcely noticing her surroundings, Shannon pulled off her clothes and got into bed, falling almost immediately into a deep, dreamless sleep.

CHAPTER SIX

SHANNON was awoken the next morning by the maid bringing her tea on a silver tray. Sipping it slowly, propped up on the pillows, Shannon took stock of her surroundings. The room could have come straight out of the pages of a fashionable magazine: Every Woman's Dream of a Perfect Bedroom. The frilled bedspread and hangings on the fourposter bed matched the daintily flowered wallpaper; the kidney-shaped dressing table was also frilled and beribboned. The carpet was a plush white, while a huge bowl of white roses rested on the mahogany bureau and ruffled white curtains were looped across the windowpanes. Somehow it was exactly what Shannon would have expected.

She poured herself another cup of tea from the miniature silver teapot. The gold clock, decorated with plump and smiling cupids, that stood on the mantel had already told her it was nine-thirty, so she knew Rick—and probably Charles—had left for town while Louise would undoubtedly still be sleeping; that left her, Shannon, to her own devices for the rest of the morning, and she was grateful for this. Rick . . . she stared unseeingly at the far wall, her green eyes very thoughtful. If it was true about Lorna's intervention in their lives, then he had broken their engagement with the best of motives—did that mean that he still loved her? He had kissed her last night, hadn't he? A year ago, even six months ago, she would have given anything for that kiss. Why then had she felt nothing last night? No pleasure or desire . . . . equally no revulsion. Just nothing. Perhaps he was right and she had been overtired.

There came to her nostrils the faint elusive fragrance of the roses on the bureau. Blaise had given her roses, although red ones, not white. She had never been in-different when Blaise had kissed her. But Blaise had gone away and left her and had not bothered to get in touch with her since . . . even though she had been in this house less than twenty-four hours, she already sensed that there was no place for Blaise in it. His father's barely disguised enmity, his stepmother's indifference, his half-brother's rivalry—none of his family harboured friendly or wel-coming emotions towards Blaise. Why not? Was it their fault? Or was it his? He had gone back on his word to her; perhaps he had done the same thing to his family so many times that they no longer depended on him, and consequently no longer were concerned for him, or worried about his absences. Puzzled, and made obscurely unhappy by this train of thought, Shannon could never-theless see that it would dovetail with the facts as she knew them. And this made her unhappier still. . . .

Impulsively she got out of bed, reaching for her house-coat and slippers. Last night Louise had made it clear that Blaise's room was in this wing of the house; maybe there she would gain some clue to the personality of the man whom she had never seen and who in so many ways was a stranger to her, yet who had briefly and momen-tarily been closer to her than anyone else in her life.

The hallway was deserted, no sounds penetrating from

other parts of the house. Pushing open the next three doors, Shannon only discovered what were obviously other guestrooms, and a luxuriously fitted bathroom. There was only one door left, the one at the farthest end of the corridor, and hence the most remote from the rest of the house. Stifling an absurd instinct to knock, Shannon quietly pushed it open and slipped inside, letting it close behind her.

Instantly she knew her search was ended, and she had a strange sense of coming home, of being welcomed, that she had not experienced anywhere else at Hardwoods. This room was not afraid to express the personality of the owner, she thought—and a complex and subtle personality it was. The antique Bessarabian carpet had the muted, iridescent tones of a dove's breast; pearl grey and soft shades of brown. Three walls had been painted the same pearl grey, while the bed was covered in supple, tawny suede. The fourth wall was entirely composed of built-in bookshelves, laden with what she could already see was an intriguing and cosmopolitan collection of titles. A teak cabinet filled with pottery stood between the two windows that had as their view the fields, the silver band of the river, and the gently rolling hills.

She had hoped she might find a photograph of Blaise, even a school picture or a university grouping; but the only photograph, silver-framed, was of a woman. A beautiful woman with high cheekbones and haunting deep-set eyes, her hair a blonde swathe about her proudly held head—Blaise's mother, it had to be, Shannon knew intuitively, wishing the black and white image could come to life and describe the mystery that was her son.

Taking her time, Shannon picked out a book to read and then dressed and went downstairs. She sat in the garden for a while, she ate a delicious lunch in company with Louise who then departed to visit a friend, she chatted with Sam as he polished the car. In the afternoon she slept for a while, then showered and changed into a narrow-fitting teal blue dress of very fine wool and her prettiest high-heeled shoes.

That Rick appreciated the trouble she had gone to was evident as she entered the living room. 'Wow!' he exclaimed boyishly. 'It's worth driving from town for that!' As though it was his right, he walked over to her and kissed her full on the mouth. 'How are you, honey? You look much more rested—did you have a nice day?'

He looked very handsome and flatteringly pleased to see her, so that her smile was perhaps warmer than she intended. 'A lovely day, thank you—sinfully lazy!'

'I'm sure that's what you needed. Can I get you something to drink—how about a sherry?'

He could not have been a more pleasant companion during the meal and she felt herself warming towards him. Afterwards, Charles and Louise had been invited out to play bridge and took their leave. 'You wouldn't believe it, but Mother's a very good bridge player,' Rick remarked. 'She looks so absentminded that the opposition always underestimates her!' Shannon smiled diplomatically, being under no illusions about Louise. 'So now I've got you to myself—what would you like to do? If you want to get out of the house for a while, we could go for a drive.'

In front of her eyes flashed the nightmare vision of a truck racing towards them and visibly she flinched. 'No, I—I don't think so.'

He put his arms around her, his face very close to hers. 'Darling, I'm sorry. Do you think I've ever forgotten that the accident was my fault—or ever forgiven myself? Believe me, I've mended my ways since then.'

Her eyes fell. It *had* been his fault, and it had left her with a deep, superstitious dread of ever driving with him again. 'I'd still rather not, Rick,' she murmured.

'Could-n't we go for a walk instead?'

'It was starting to rain as I got home.'

Shannon liked walking in the rain; Rick obviously did not. 'I know—why don't we see if Sam would like to go into town with us?' she suggested. 'We could double date with him and Lisa—you'd like her, I'm sure.'

'Honey,' Rick said forbearingly, 'Sam's the chauffeur.'

For a moment she thought he was joking. 'So what?' she said blankly.

He lit a cigarette with an irritable snap of his lighter. 'I'm not in the habit of being seen in public with a chauffeur and his two-bit girl-friend.'

'Sam is an honours student who'll be a credit to the legal profession and Lisa was last year's gold medallist,' she snapped. 'Besides which, they happen to be my friends.'

'You should know by now I have to pick my friends with care, Shannon.' He flicked ash into the fireplace and then straightened, passing a hand over his smooth blond hair. 'I don't want to argue with you,' he said coaxingly. 'Let's go and light the fire in the library and put on some music—we don't have to go out at all.' It was a peace-offering and reluctantly she accepted it as such, following him out of the room. 'As long as we're together, that's the main thing,' he went on. 'Tomorrow I'm afraid I have a dinner and reception to attend, then on Wednesday Mother's giving a dinner party here, so this will be our only chance to be alone for a while.'

Not knowing how to respond to this, Shannon wandered over to examine the bookshelves, where neat sets of gold-embossed books stood in undisturbed rows. Soon flames were crackling in the hearth, while Barbra Streisand began to croon seductively about love. Rick was just dimming the lights when Shannon exclaimed, 'Wait a moment, Rick—these are family photos, aren't they?'

'That's right,' he answered, not sounding very interested.

Shannon looked more closely at the group of pictures mounted on the oak panelling: Charles and Louise in the garden, Rick playing tennis, Louise and Charles and Rick in a more formal pose, and finally Rick as a teenager sitting on the front steps. That was all. Swallowing her disappointment, she said, 'Blaise lived in this house, didn't he? Why aren't there any of him?'

'He left home at sixteen.'

'He did?' She turned to face Rick, the firelight dancing on her face. 'Why?'

'I don't know,' was the impatient reply. 'I guess he was always a loner, and never made much of an effort to fit in. I don't think Dad ever forgave him for leaving, though.'

Shannon stared in frustration at the smiling faces in the photographs, knowing she could get from them no more answers than she had from Rick. 'How long before he came back?'

'Ten years, maybe. Even now, he rarely stays here more than a week at a time.'

'Does he have a home of his own?'

'He owns a place off in the woods somewhere north of Toronto—I've never been there, so I'm not sure just where.'

'Has anyone bothered to phone there to see if he got back from his trip?'

'Of course not,' Rick growled. 'Why the hell should they?'

'He does happen to be a member of your family.'

'Will you stop harping on Blaise, Shannon!' Rick exploded.

In complete frustration she cried, 'No one in this house will even talk about him, that's what gets me. What did he ever do to deserve being ostracised like that?'

'Since you're the only one who's interested, you'd better ask him next time you see him.'

'You're forgetting, Rick,' she answered with deadly sarcasm, 'I've *never* seen him.' Rick stared at her blankly for a minute before her meaning penetrated and it gave her the time to regret her hasty words. 'I'm sorry, Rick, I shouldn't have said that. But you do see why I'm interested in seeing even a photograph of him? He changed my life for me—and so far I haven't even been able to thank him because nobody seems to know or care where he is.'

'Okay,' he said heavily. 'And I'm sorry I lost my cool. It just seems as though you'd done nothing but ask questions about Blaise since you got here and I was getting a bit tired of it.'

'Truce,' she said lightly, no longer wanting to quarrel with him even though she knew none of her questions had been answered and she was no nearer to solving the enigma that Blaise presented than she had ever been.

'Come and sit down by the fire,' said Rick, patting the chesterfield 'I finalised a really fantastic deal today and I want to tell you about it.'

She sat beside him, her eyes trained on the fire's constant, hypnotic movement as he talked, making an effort to show some interest in a subject that, she realised with a little jolt of dismay, did not really interest her at all. Yet it was a major part of Rick's life—and it was Rick whom she had loved. Still did love, according to Blaise. Her green eyes troubled, she glanced up to find him staring at her.

'You're so beautiful,' he said huskily. 'More beautiful than you were a year ago. You have no idea how much I've missed you, Shannon.'

'And I you,' she replied quietly, for it was the literal truth. 'I often wondered why you couldn't at least have come and visited me.'

He shook his head. 'Your mother made me promise not to; she thought it would only unsettle you.'

All very logical, and no doubt true. But Shannon could not help thinking that no consideration had stopped Blaise: he had made up his mind to see her and he had let nothing—and no one—stand in his way.

'Did you really miss me, honey?' Rick was asking, his hand caressing her shoulder.

'Of course I did,' she answered absently, remembering how Blaise had told her mother he would tear the house apart brick by brick if Lorna refused him admittance.

'I'm glad you did. Because it means you still cared for me,' he said softly, sliding his hand under her hair and pulling her towards him with surprising strength.

She blinked, coming back to the present with a start. 'Rick——'

He silenced any protest she might have made by kissing her with considerable expertise, ignoring the tension in her body and her lack of response. When he raised his head, there was fire in his pale eyes. 'Relax and enjoy it,' he said thickly. 'No one's going to disturb us here.'

She tried, for after all this was Rick, and not that long ago she would have given almost anything to find herself in his arms. As he began kissing her again, she willed herself to relax, letting her hands slide around his neck and making her mouth move under his. But it didn't work. There was none of the piercing sweetness that Blaise's kisses had evoked, no pulse of desire. Instead she began to feel that she would suffocate if she didn't get free. Her heart pounding in her ears, she wrenched her head away. 'Please, Rick, don't!' she gasped.

Accidentally—or was it accidentally?—his hand slid along the curve of her breast. 'I love you, Shannon—I never stopped loving you.'

Somehow she had to end this. As calmly as she could,

she said, 'Rick, this is all too much for me. Remember I was on my own for the year I was blind, and now I'm only just getting used to having my sight back—it's far too soon for me to know how I feel about you. Goodness, we've only spent a few hours together!'

'I don't blame you for playing hard to get after the way I broke off our engagement.'

Exasperated, she said, 'I'm not playing any kind of a game with you, Rick, or trying to punish you. I'm just —confused, and I don't want to be rushed, that's all.' She shifted her position on the chesterfield to put space between them.

'I need a drink.' He went over to the built-in bar, and added with rather bad grace, 'Do you want one?'

'No, thank you.'

Pouring a liberal amount of whisky in a glass, he added a couple of ice cubes. 'So where do we go from here?'

'Can't we just enjoy each other's company for a while? Get to know each other again? After all, I'm going to be here for nearly three weeks.'

'I suppose so,' he said grudgingly. 'I don't seem to have much choice, do I?'

Thoroughly out of sympathy with him, she made an effort to change the subject. 'Tell me about this dinner party—am I invited?'

'Of course you are. I told Mother you'd be my partner for the evening. There'll be about twenty people, I think —my boss and his wife, Gerald and Joan Thurston; some of Dad's political friends and business associates; a couple of mother's cronies. I want you to make a good impression on Gerald, he's beginning to hint that it's time I settled down.'

They were back to square one, she thought rebelliously. 'My mother saw to it that I have very good manners,' she said limpidly. 'I promise I'll behave myself.'

As it happened, it was an effort to do so as far as Gerald and Joan Thurston were concerned. They were among the first guests to arrive and immediately cornered Shannon. Gerald was short and stout and pompous with a tendency to touch her rather more than she liked; his wife, lacquered and polished to an astonishing degree even in that sophisticated crowd, had the coldest eyes Shannon had ever seen, coupled with a memory like a computer for all the interrelationships of the 'best' families. She soon established to her own satisfaction that Shannon's pedigree was acceptable and then lost interest, wandering off in the direction of the bar and thereby leaving Shannon to Gerald's undivided attentions. Fastening a pudgy hand on her bare arm, he looked her up and down appreciatively. Shannon had spent the best part of the previous morning selecting the dress she was wearing, having been driven to Ottawa by Sam; in the shop the rounded neckline and empire waistline had not seemed immodest in any way, but now she had the uncomfortable feeling that rather too much bare skin was showing.

'You look charming, my dear,' Gerald wheezed. 'Rick's a very fortunate young man. He was telling me of the tragedy of your broken engagement, and now I'm delighted to see you back together again. A fine young man—he'll go far.' He paused suggestively, lighting a short, fat cigar with a series of asthmatic puffs. 'Would I be premature to congratulate you?'

'You would,' she said shortly.

'Take my advice and don't wait too long. He's quite a catch, is Rick, and you wouldn't want him to slip through your fingers.'

Odious little man, she thought crossly, wishing someone would rescue her. Fortunately Charles caught her look of appeal and brought them into a larger group. For Shannon the evening became something of a strain,

for she still tired easily, the smoke bothered her eyes, and
a lot of the conversation was a kind of in-group gossip
in which she could not participate. Finally, however, the
last guests were ushered out of the door. With a theatrical
sigh Louise declared she would have to rest for two days
to recover, and goodhumouredly Charles followed her
out of the room, leaving Rick and Shannon alone in the
normally tidy living room now littered with ashtrays and
empty glasses.

'Gerald and Joan really took to you, Shannon,' Rick
said eagerly. 'You must have said all the right things.'

Shannon could not imagine Joan taking to anyone,
but forbore to say so. 'He seemed to think our re-
engagement was a fait accompli.'

'Well, it is, isn't it, darling?' Rick smiled indulgently
and for the first time she realised he must have had
rather a lot to drink. 'I don't blame you for keeping me
on tenterhooks for a while, but I know you'll come around
in the end.'

'I wish you weren't so sure,' she said slowly. 'Because
I'm not. . . .' Disturbed, she gazed up at his flushed, handsome face. He was ambitious and wealthy and charming,
and not long ago she had been in love with him—so
what was the matter with her now?

He came over to her and slid his arms around her
waist, gently rocking her back and forth. 'I'll get down
on my knees when I propose to you if that will make you
feel better!' He must have seen the flicker of exaspera-
tion that crossed the clear green eyes, for he sobered
abruptly. 'Seriously, Shannon, I'm more in love with
you now than I've ever been—and I want to make you
my wife. Will you marry me, honey?'

Not even giving herself time to think, knowing she had
to trust her instincts, she gasped without any finesse,
'Rick, I can't. Not now.'

Not until she had spoken did she realise how sure of

her he had been. His face darkened. 'What do you mean
—not now?' he demanded.

She shrugged helplessly. 'I'm just not ready to make
that kind of commitment.'

'You were ready enough a year ago.'

'I know. But a lot's happened to me in that year. And
one of the things I had to learn was to get along without
you. I can't just reverse that process overnight. Please—
you've got to give me time, Rick.'

He stepped back, releasing her, and in a very charac-
teristic gesture smoothed down his hair. 'You really *have*
changed, haven't you?'

'Of course I have—it was inevitable.'

His features hardened. 'I think there's more here than
meets the eye—did something happen between you and
Blaise?'

Into her mind came the sound of the robins on the hillside where Blaise had kissed her; in five earth-shattering
minutes he had taught her more about the passion that
can flare between man and woman than she had ever
known before. She had hesitated a split second too long,
and Rick grabbed her by the shoulders. 'I was right—
something did happen, didn't it? Tell me the truth,
Shannon.'

'A couple of things happened,' she said steadily. 'He
kissed me, yes. I don't have to apologise to you or anyone
else for that. I was—and am—free to kiss whomever I
please.' His fingers dug into her arm and she saw he
was about to speak. 'You're hurting me, and I'm not
finished yet. Because Blaise told me two things I couldn't
understand. First, that you didn't have a picture of me
to show him, and secondly that you'd told him we'd
made love. I gave you a framed photograph of myself
for your birthday, remember? And you know as well as
I do that we never made love.' She scanned his face,
seeing his eyes narrow and his mouth tighten. 'Why did

you lie to him, Rick?'

He turned away from her impatiently, reaching for a cigarette in the silver canister on the coffee table. 'Blaise has always had a way with women,' he burst out. 'When he told me he was flying out west to see you, I was afraid of what he might do. I thought if I told him we'd made love, he'd realise you were mine and keep his hands off you.' Swiftly he moved from defence to attack. 'But it didn't work, did it, Shannon?'

'No,' she said, with all the bitterness of Blaise's broken promises in her voice. 'It just made him think I was easy game.'

'And were you?'

She flushed scarlet. 'I'll tell you what I told him—I've never made love with anyone in my life!'

His eyes raked the slender lines of her figure. 'I'm the one who's going to make love to you, Shannon—not Blaise. Is that clear?'

She was trembling and the colour had drained from her face. His question was unanswerable, she knew, so she countered it with one of her own. 'And the photograph?'

He rubbed his forehead. 'Breaking our engagement was the hardest thing I ever did in my life. Afterwards I couldn't stand to look at it because it only reminded me of all I'd lost.' He grinned ruefully. 'I hate to tell you this, because it sounds so damned theatrical—and I certainly would never have told Blaise, he'd have laughed his head off—but I threw it in the river.'

'Oh.' Shannon sat down abruptly. 'Rick, I certainly don't want you thinking I'm in love with Blaise—you do understand that, don't you?'

A cool nod. 'If you say so.'

'But as far as you and I are concerned, I must have more time. Please?'

Because the light was behind him and his face shadowed, she missed the lightning-swift calculation that crossed his eyes. Swiftly he walked over to her, raising her to her feet, his smile full of a boyish, unforced charm. 'Of course, honey. You're well worth waiting for, don't you know that?'

In sudden gratitude she rested her forehead on his chest and he held her gently. 'You'd better go to bed,' he murmured. 'You must be exhausted.'

Touched by his concern, she kissed him quickly, a featherlight brush of her lips on his mouth. 'Bless you— you really do understand, don't you? Goodnight, and I'll see you tomorrow.'

Over the next few days it did seem as though Rick had finally accepted her need for more time. He was once again the pleasant, lighthearted companion he had been when they first met, making her laugh, bringing her extravagant presents, falling in with all her wishes. When he had to make a week-long business trip to Vancouver, she found herself missing his company, more particularly so since Charles and Louise were spending a few days at a friend's summer resort in Thousand Islands. She was feeling much stronger now, and every day went for a long walk in the woods and fields that surrounded the house; her skin was lightly tanned and she had gained back the weight she had lost in hospital. And always there was the incredible miracle of being able to see . . . if it had not been for the constant underlying unease she felt about Blaise, she would have been perfectly content.

Running lightly up the steps two days after Rick had left, she let herself in the front door in time to hear the phone ring. Stepton, the impressively dignified butler, answered it. 'Hardwoods. Stepton speaking . . . I beg your pardon? . . . Who is speaking, please? . . .' A long silence and unconsciously Shannon found herself waiting for the next response. 'Where are you, sir?' She tensed, for the butler's voice had been shaken from its usual imperturbable calm. '*Where?* . . . Just stay right there, sir. I'll send Blakeney to get you. . . . Did you hear me, sir? Mr Strathern . . .?' Slowly Stepton put down the receiver.

'What's wrong?' Shannon asked, unable to hide her concern.

Stepton seemed at a loss for words. 'I—I don't know. It was Mr Strathern——'

'Rick?'

'No, no—Master Blaise.'

Her heart gave a great thud. 'Where is he? Is he all right?'

'As far as I could tell, he's at the railway station.'

Stepton's rheumy grey eyes were genuinely worried; it was the first time since she had come to Hardwoods that Shannon had seen anyone care about Blaise's welfare at all, and she warmed to the old butler. Putting her hand on his black-clad arm, she asked, 'What's he doing there?'

Glancing at her, Stepton said in a hushed whisper as though someone else might be listening, 'He's either very drunk or else he's sick. I could hardly understand him. I said I'd send Blakeney to get him.'

'I'll go with him.'

'Oh, no, miss, that wouldn't be suitable——'

Shannon brushed aside his protests. 'Where's the station?'

'Blakeney knows. But, miss——'

However, Shannon had already gone, letting herself out of the front door and running towards the big garage, over which Sam had a small, self-contained apartment. He was tinkering with the motor of Rick's sports car, and straightened when he saw her coming. 'Don't rush around like that—it's too hot,' he said goodhumouredly, for it was unseasonably warm for June.

'Sam, Blaise just phoned—he's at the station. Stepton thinks there's something wrong. Can we go right now?'

One look at her face and he grabbed his shirt from a hook on the wall and pulled it on over his grease-stained singlet. 'Sure—but what the hell's he doing at the station?'

'I don't know—hurry, Sam!'

'Okay, okay, keep your hair on. We'll take the Chevrolet. Come on.'

He accelerated down the driveway. Automatically putting on her dark glasses, Shannon asked, 'How far do we have to go?'

'About five miles—we'll be there in ten minutes. Why did Stepton think something was wrong?'

'He said Blaise was either drunk or ill.'

'Well, we'll soon find out, so just relax, okay?'

An understanding friendship had sprung up between them since Shannon had come to Hardwoods, and now Shannon said feelingly, very glad to have him with her, 'Easier said than done.'

The station was an unimportant country stopover, one set of tracks, one small orange-painted building with a paved yard surrounded by trees. There were no signs of life. Sam pulled up by the side of the road and they both got out, Shannon looking around her uncertainly.

Everything drowsed in the sunshine. There was no wind and the leaves hung still on the trees. Even the birds were quiet. A peaceful, sleepy scene, yet Shannon's heart was racing in her breast and she was suddenly desperately afraid. She grabbed Sam's arm. 'Where would he be?'

'There's a waiting room at the front. Come along.'

She was still holding his arm as they went around the corner of the building; not watching where she was going, she tripped over a tussock of grass that had poked up between a crack in the pavement.

A man had been leaning against the wall facing the tracks; he must have heard their footsteps, for he was watching for their approach. He saw a brown-haired girl in a peasant skirt and embroidered blouse, dark glasses hiding her eyes. She was holding on to the arm of a sturdy young man and even as he watched, she tripped and stumbled.

The colour drained from his face. With a palpable effort he straightened, trying to stand without the support of the wall. 'Shannon——' he said harshly. 'Oh God, Shannon, the operation didn't work.'

Shannon stopped dead in her tracks. It was the voice that had, she now realised, haunted her for the past month and a half: Blaise had come home. Deliberately she let go of Sam's arm and took off her dark glasses, her eyes the green of the trees behind her. Holding herself straight, she began to walk towards him, skirting the luggage trolley that someone had left by the wall. She stopped scarcely a foot away from him. 'Bridget was right,' she said quietly. 'Your eyes are the colour of the sky.'

For a moment she thought he was going to fall, and she grabbed his elbows. 'Thank God,' he muttered. 'I thought it hadn't worked—that I'd made you go through all that for nothing.'

He was sagging against her, his eyes closed, and she called, 'Sam! Come and help!'

'He's not drunk—he's ill,' Sam said crisply. 'We'd better get him home as quick as we can. Wait here with him, Shannon. I'll bring the car round.'

For a moment she and Blaise were alone together in the somnolent afternoon sunshine. The girl's eyes roamed his face and it was almost as though every feature was already known to her: the strongly carved profile, the firm chin and broad forehead, now beaded with sweat, under an untidy thatch of sun-streaked blond hair. His eyes were sunk deep in their sockets, while patches of hectic colour stained his cheeks. He was leaning back against the wall again, and she reached up to touch his face; his skin felt dry and burningly hot, the stubble of beard rough against her fingers.

Then there was the sound of tyres on the pavement, and Sam was beside her, looping one of Blaise's arms across his shoulders. 'You take the other side, Shannon. I've put the seat down in the back—we'll put him there.' Blaise was a dead weight, and Shannon was breathing hard by the time they accomplished this. Blaise's head lolled sideways and in sudden terror she knew he had no idea where he was or where they were taking him.

'Let's hurry, Sam,' she said raggedly.

'Yeah. . . .' It was just as well they met no police cars on the way home, for Sam, although he drove with concentrated skill, broke every speed restriction there was. He pulled up as near to the front door as he could get and jumped out. 'I'll go and get Stepton—stay here.'

Blaise was unconscious now, his breathing quick and shallow. Using a fireman's hold, the two men lifted him out of the car and carried him into the house. 'We might as well take him straight to his own room,' Sam said authoritatively. 'Shannon, the name of the family doctor is on the pad by the phone—see if you can reach him.'

She hurried to do as she was bid, although her fingers were shaking badly enough that she had trouble dialling. The receptionist put her through to the doctor who, after she had described Blaise's condition, said with a very comforting lack of excitement, 'Probably a recurrence of malaria—it's happened to him before. I was just starting for home, so I'll drop in on the way. Say fifteen minutes.'

Somewhat reassured, Shannon started upstairs, passing Stepton on the way. 'How is he?' she said anxiously.

'Conscious again, miss, but very restless.'

She ran up the rest of the stairs and down the corridor to the end room. Blaise was in bed, wearing a pair of dark silk pyjamas. His eyes flew to the door as she pushed it open. 'Shannon,' he said, his voice weak but completely lucid. 'I wasn't dreaming that you could see again?'

She favoured him with a brilliant smile as she went over to the bed and unselfconsciously sat down on the edge of it, scarcely even noticing Sam's, 'Call me if you need anything,' as he slipped out of the room. 'No, you weren't dreaming, Blaise. Dr MacAuley says I may have to wear glasses for reading—I'll find out when I go back for a check-up—but other than that everything's fine.'

'Good,' was all he said, but some of the tension seemed to leave his body. He was pale now where he had been flushed before and even as she watched he was shaken by a bout of shivering. 'You're cold!' she exclaimed.

'Don't worry—it's always like this. Although not often this bad.'

'Dr Saunders will be here shortly. He mentioned malaria,' she said tentatively.

'That's right—I spent a couple of years in Africa.'

'There's a lot I don't know about you,' she said, and then blushed at her presumption.

However, he was in no state to notice, for he was futilely trying to control the shivers that racked his body. His teeth were clenched; the hand that was outside the covers was white-knuckled with strain. Not even stopping to think, Shannon took it within both of hers, rubbing it to try and give it warmth. He gripped her fingers with bruising strength. 'Don't go away, will you?' he muttered.

Tears pricked at her eyes and she blinked them back furiously. He was normally a man both vigorous and independent, she knew, and that he should be reduced to clutching her hand like a child sent a wave of compassion through her. 'I'll stay as long as you need me,' she promised. It was doubtful whether he heard her, but he maintained his grip on her hand as though it were a lifeline, and with that she was content.

Dr Saunders was a dapper little man, his scant hair carefully combed for maximum effect, a spotless white silk handkerchief tucked into his pocket. But his movements were quick and sure, and his eyes, of an indeterminable shade of grey, both shrewd and kindly. 'Now let go of her hand, Blaise,' he said. 'She can come back after I've had a look at you.'

'Hi, Doc,' Blaise said weakly. 'Sorry about this.'

Shannon left the room feeling obscurely comforted, for she sensed that Dr Saunders, like Stepton, was glad to see Blaise at Hardwoods again, perhaps more glad than his family would be. She wandered up and down the corridor; the doctor seemed to be taking a very long time. Eventually, however, he emerged from Blaise's room. His expression was sober and she said uneasily, 'How is he?'

'Are Charles and Louise home?'

'No—they're away for a week.'

'I see. Have you ever done any nursing?' She shook her head. Her growing anxiety must have shown in her face for he said, 'He's in rather worse shape than I expected and I'm just wondering if I should try and get him admitted to hospital. Trouble is, the place is jam-packed already, and it would probably be more restful for him to be at home.'

Briefly he outlined what she would have to do, and she said eagerly, 'I'm sure I could manage that.' She hesitated. 'Is it a worse attack than usual?'

'I think the accident weakend his resistance—doesn't look as though he's been taking care of himself at all.'

'Accident?' she repeated, puzzled.

'So he didn't tell you—typical of Blaise, always was close-mouthed about his troubles.'

'What accident?' she demanded.

'Oh, apparently about a week after he got there one of the crew went out on the rocks to photograph the sea during a storm. He was washed into the water and would have drowned, I gather, if Blaise hadn't jumped in after him. Unfortunately Blaise got the worst of it—the sea drove him against the rocks, and he came out of it with bruised ribs, and a nasty gash on his leg that pretty well immobilised him. Lost a lot of blood into the bargain.'

She stared at him, her face very pale. 'That explains why he didn't come and see me,' she whispered. 'But why didn't he let me know?'

'Two reasons, I would suspect,' the doctor said, a twinkle in his eye. 'For one thing they were stuck up in the wilderness miles from anywhere. No roads, no post office, and certainly no telephones. And secondly, Blaise has been used to a singular lack of interest in both his accomplishments and his problems over the years— to tell his parents about the accident wouldn't occur to him.'

Shannon let out her breath in a long sigh. Despite her concern about Blaise's illness, she felt a mingling of relief and happiness well up within her: his long silence was explained. And now he was home. . . .

The doctor was checking his watch. 'I'd better get going. Call me at home this evening if he seems to get any worse. Otherwise I'll drop by first thing tomorrow on the way to the hospital.'

She smiled gratefully. 'Thank you. Goodbye, Dr Saunders.'

The next few hours were uneventful, for Blaise had drifted into an uneasy sleep. Stepton brought a cot from one of the spare bedrooms and made it up for her in Blaise's room; Sam relieved her so she could eat supper. 'Call me if you need any help in the night,' he ordered. 'You're sure you can handle this?'

'Yes.' Knowing Sam would understand, she said, 'It

seems the least I can do for him, Sam, because if it wasn't for him I'd still be blind. Sitting day after day in my mother's house—he rescued me from all that.'

'So it's gratitude you feel towards him?'

Remembering those kisses on the hillside, she blushed slightly, avoiding his eyes. 'Well, of course.'

He grinned and patted her shoulder. 'Whatever you say. Don't let yourself get overtired, though, Shannon—he, I'm sure, would disapprove of that. 'Night!'

She had made a good friend in Sam, Shannon thought, as she went to her own room and changed into her night-dress and a long robe of dark green velour. She remembered Rick's refusal to associate with Sam and winced away from the memory; at the moment Rick seemed very far away. Back in Blaise's room, she saw that he was still asleep, the soft golden lamplight shadowing his sunken cheeks and bruised eye sockets. To be able to see him at last seemed a miracle, and for a long time she sat quietly by the bed, her eyes rarely leaving him; it was as though she was trying to get beneath the surface to the man within, a man who was still an enigma to her. Hated by Rick, ignored by his parents . . . dictatorial and demanding . . . yet now made vulnerable and helpless by illness and exhaustion.

At eleven she dimmed the bedside lamp to its lowest level, took off her housecoat, and settled herself on the narrow cot, certain she would hear him if he called. The shadowed room was as friendly and welcoming as it had seemed on her first visit and she was aware of a deep contentment to be where she was. She belonged here, she thought drowsily, and sleep claimed her before she could examine any of the implications of this.

CHAPTER SEVEN

SOMEONE was moaning as though in pain—an ugly sound, harsh and repetitious. Wondering if she was dreaming, confused by the unfamiliar bed, Shannon pushed herself up on one elbow. Three-thirty, the tiny gold hands of her watch said. She rubbed her eyes and suddenly became fully awake as she remembered where she was and who was in the room with her. Swiftly she got out of bed and went over to him. His eyes were shut, while from his throat came the sound that had awakened her; his forehead felt ice-cold and as she rested a hand on his shoulder, she could feel the bone-deep shudders through his big frame.

He must have sensed her presence. His eyelids flickered, and dazed blue eyes fastened themselves on her. 'Shannon?'

She squeezed his shoulder gently. 'Yes, I'm here.'

'I thought you'd gone,' he muttered. From beneath the covers he brought his hand up to cover hers. 'You feel so warm.'

His fingers were cold too, she realised in dismay. With her free hand she pulled up the eiderdown to cover him, tucking it around his body. But he was still shaken by uncontrollable tremors, and in a gesture that touched her to the heart, he laid his cheek against the palm of her hand, as though savouring its warmth and mutely grateful for its comfort.

She hesitated only momentarily. Reaching over, she switched off the bedside light. Then she lifted the covers and slid into bed beside him. Not giving herself time to think, she curved her body to his, throwing one leg

104

across him and drawing him closer with her arm; he was so cold he seemed to drain all the heat from her limbs.

She felt the shock run through him. 'Shannon, you mustn't——'

'Hush,' she whispered. 'It's all right, Blaise, it's the only way to warm you. Lie still.' Imperceptibly he relaxed, and slowly her body heat began to seep into his chest and legs, and the fits of shivering became less frequent and less violent.

It was very quiet in the room, for there was only the sound of their mingled breathing. As her eyes grew accustomed to the dark, Shannon was able to discern the outlines of the furniture and the glimmer of the silver-framed photograph on the bureau; closer still she could see the untidy thatch of fair hair, the strong bones of his face, the rise and fall of his broad chest. She had never lain so intimately with a man before, and a new warmth pulsed its way along her veins; he was so big, his frame solid and big-boned where hers was all softness and curves. As though he had read her mind his hand moved from her shoulder to her waist and then to the small of her back, drawing her closer. With a lazy sensuality he buried his face in her throat, where the skin was smooth and delicately scented, and where the pulse fluttered like the wings of a trapped butterfly. Innocent though she was, she had to know she was arousing him, and her blood began to beat to the same primitive rhythm as his lips wandered along the slender whiteness of her neck and by an unspoken consent found her parted lips. She should have felt frightened—or at least shy. But, perhaps because of the enveloping darkness, or perhaps because of the silent sureness of his hands and mouth, she felt neither of these; rather, her heart was singing in her breast. Trustingly she kissed him back and equally trustingly her body moulded itself to his. He murmured something against her skin. 'What did you say?' she whispered.

His answer was to push the straps of her nightgown from her shoulders, and then his head was in the valley between her breasts and nothing she had ever felt in her life prepared her for the flooding sweetness that banished thought and prudence and control. Her fingers awkward with haste, she undid the jacket of his pyjamas and beneath her palms felt the sinewed flatness, the tangled hair, of his chest.

Time lost its meaning as they held each other close. Eventually Blaise raised his head and said huskily, 'You're so beautiful, Shannon.' His lips traced the delicate line of her cheek. 'So warm and soft and lovely.'

Although he did not say that they had to stop what they were doing, nevertheless by some silent communication they drew a little apart from each other and the tumult of her heartbeat slowly subsided. Blaise's head dropped to her shoulder and she cradled it there, expressing through her hands all the tenderness she was feeling. His eyelids dropped shut and gradually his breathing became deep and regular as he fell asleep in her arms. She could see the lines of exhaustion seaming his cheeks, that under the year-round tan of a man who spent much time outdoors, were without colour. She was afraid if she tried to go back to her own bed she might wake him, and she knew she could not bear to do this; so she lay still, savouring a physical closeness beyond anything she had ever known . . . giving a tiny sigh of pure contentment, she nestled her face into the pillow, feeling the weight of his head at her breast and the lean length of his body lying beside her. Totally relaxed, deeply happy, she drifted off to sleep.

Someone was shaking her so roughly that her head flopped backwards and her eyes flew open. The soft grey light of dawn had seeped into the room while she slept, and as she struggled to free herself from the webs of a profound and dreamless sleep, she saw a pair of blazing blue eyes, fired by an anger so intense that instinctively she tried to draw back. But the same hands that had been shaking her refused to release her. Helpless, terrified, she stuttered, 'Blaise—what's wrong?'

'What the hell are you doing in my bed?'

'You were cold, so I got into bed to try and warm you.'

'My God, Shannon——'

An indefinable note in the harsh voice suddenly made her ashamed of an action that up until now had felt perfectly natural, and scarlet colour flooded her cheeks. 'You woke me in the night,' she tried to explain. 'I was frightened because you seemed so cold. That's all— nothing happened.'

'I'm capable of remembering that much,' he said grimly. 'Although as I recall, I got the distinct impression you might not have been unwilling.'

Humiliated that he could cheapen an intimacy that had been like a revelation to her, she choked, 'That's a hateful thing to say!'

'I don't feel particularly kindly towards you at the moment—I find myself wondering what excuse you used to insinuate yourself into Rick's bed.'

'I never did,' she said fiercely. 'I told you that! He was lying to you when he said I'd made love with him.'

'Sure,' Blaise answered sarcastically. 'Why should he bother to lie about a thing like that?'

'Because he knew you were going to visit me, and he wanted you to think he had a claim on me.'

'That sounds like the tortuous way Rick's mind would work.' He added silkily, 'And does he have a claim on you?'

For the first time Shannon hesitated, the uncertainty

in her voice mirrored in her shadowed green eyes. 'No, of course not.'

'You don't sound very sure.'

His fingers were digging into her arms like claws. 'You're hurting me, Blaise.'

'Not as much as I'd like to.'

Her eyes sought his with a kind of desperate enquiry. 'Why are you so angry?' she whispered.

With startling suddeness he flung her back on the pillows, her hair a tangle of dark silk. Momentarily his body hovered over her like some great bird of prey, cutting out from her sight everything but a pair of merciless blue eyes, and then his mouth fastened on hers. It was a kiss without tenderness or restraint; terror-stricken, she tried to free herself, but his weight pinioned her to the bed. Her blood pounded in her ears and she knew if she did not soon get air she would faint . . . then Blaise threw himself off her and she saw the same pounding of blood in the pulse at his throat and heard the harsh intake of his breath. 'And now get out of my bed, Shannon—unless, of course, you want Stepton or one of the maids to find you here.'

Shamed and ravaged and bitterly hurt, she took refuge in anger. 'Your caveman tactics don't impress me at all,' she said bitterly. 'Perhaps you should consider taking a lesson or two in technique from Rick.'

He said with deadly quietness, 'You little bitch—get out of my room.'

Shannon scrambled out of bed and the cool grey morning light shone through the thin folds of her nylon nightgown, silhouetting the slim lines of her figure. Her hands unsteady, she grabbed her housecoat from the cot, swinging it over her shoulders, and fled from the room.

The dainty artificiality of her own room at least offered some kind of refuge. She shut the door behind her and leaned back against the panels, her face very pale, all her feelings lacerated. Although through the square panes of the window she could see the gentle sweep of fields and hills, the quiet pastoral beauty of her surroundings only served to emphasize the confusion in her mind. Blaise was like a storm, she thought fancifully, a violent summer storm that would come racing up the valley; yet he was also as deep, as unfathomable and ruthless, as the sea. How could she hope to understand him? He had been tender and passionate with her; but equally he had been angry and cruel. It would almost seem as though he was jealous of Rick . . . although that would imply that Blaise wanted her for himself, and he had given no sign of that. Perhaps to attribute his behaviour to jealousy was too simple an answer. Already she sensed between the two men a deep-seated conflict rooted in the past; possibly now in the present it had caught her up in its toils.

Guesswork, she thought impatiently. All her thinking was nothing but that, just wild theorising. In unconscious frustration, her fist had been banging on the door panel behind her, and she was suddenly startled to hear a female voice say, 'Miss Hart, may I come in, please?'

Shannon swung the door open, embarrassed to find Peggy, one of the maids, standing there with the morning tea tray. 'Oh—thank you,' she murmured.

'Should I take anything to Mr Strathern, do you think?'

'No, I shouldn't—I believe he's sleeping.' At least she hoped he was, she thought with a wry twist to her mouth. One more confrontation like the last one and she'd be finished for the day. . . .

Shortly after Shannon had gone downstairs, Dr Saunders came as promised, joining her in the dining room after he had seen Blaise. Today his suit was a superbly tailored grey worsted, with a blue silk square tucked in the pocket. 'He's on the mend,' he said cheerfully. 'Constitution of an ox, that man. He should take it easy for a day or two. See what you can do, Shannon.'

Drily she responded, 'I can't imagine anyone, let alone me, stopping Blaise Strathern from doing anything that he wants to do.'

The doctor gave a bark of laughter. 'You're quite right, of course! Well, he's sleeping now and let's hope he'll have the sense to stay in bed today. If there should be any change for the worse, let me know, Shannon—otherwise, I don't think I need to come back.

Blaise did spend the day in his room, and Shannon purposefully stayed away, using as an excuse to Sam, with his far-too-discerning eyes, that she needed the rest. It was at least partly true; she felt very tired, although she knew this was more from emotional stress than from lack of sleep. After dinner she was half dozing in one of the library's comfortably padded armchairs—more conducive to sleeping than to study—when Stepton cleared his throat tactfully in the doorway. 'Er—miss?'

Shannon rubbed her eyes, smiling at him; behind his ultra-correct butler's mannerisms she had already discerned a slightly austere but nevertheless genuine friendliness, and now she said, 'It's all right, I really was awake.'

He permitted himself a faint smile. 'Yes, miss. Telephone for you—a long-distance call, the operator said.'

'Oh?' She scrambled to her feet, wondering if it could be her mother; on her arrival at Hardwoods a letter had been awaiting her from Lorna and through the neatly penned phrases Shannon had sensed the conflict between Lorna's pleasure that Shannon had recovered her sight and her dismay that her daughter was so far away from home; at least Blaise's intervention in their lives had granted Shannon some degree of insight, and hence acceptance, into the motives behind Lorna's over-possessiveness.

However, when she picked up the receiver and gave her name to the operator, it was a man's voice that greeted her. 'Hello, honey,' Rick said breezily. 'How's my favourite girl?'

She was suddenly very glad to hear from him. 'Hi, Rick—this is a nice surprise.'

'Got out of a meeting earlier than I expected and thought I'd give you a call to see how you're feeling.'

'Fine—but disgracefully lazy. How are the negotiations going?'

He described at some length the manoeuvres and complications of his latest contract, his voice still fresh and enthusiastic after what had obviously been a long day spent around the conference table. That was his world, Shannon thought, the world of finance and conglomerates and big business; a manipulative and ruthless world that to her had an air of unreality. Finally he finished. 'Sorry—I must be boring you.'

'I'm afraid this call is costing you a lot of money,' she temporised.

'So what? It's good to hear your voice.' After the see-sawing of emotions with Blaise, Shannon could not help but to appreciate his approval of her. 'Did Dad and Mother get home yet?'

'No—they're not due back for a couple of days.'

'What have you been doing with yourself since I left?'

Aware that she was nervous, and annoyed with herself for being so, she licked her lips. 'Well, as a matter of fact, it's been a bit hectic,' she said with attempted casualness. 'Blaise came back yesterday.'

A momentary silence that was loud with things unsaid. 'I see,' Rick said coldly. 'What's the matter—no more bits of pottery to dig up?'

'He was ill, Rick. He'd had a bad accident up there and injured his leg, and then he came down with a bout of malaria. We had to get Dr Saunders in yesterday.

When he came again this morning, he said Blaise was a lot better.'

'So who's looking after him?'

'Sam and Stepton,' she said evasively. 'And I've been helping, of course.'

'Why didn't he go to hospital?'

'It was full. And I was perfectly capable of doing anything that needed doing.' Remembering just what she *had* done, and Blaise's reactions, she fell silent, glad Rick could not see her face.

'When's he leaving?' he rapped.

'I don't know—he's still recuperating,' she replied with faint hauteur.

'You think I'm over-reacting, don't you, Shannon? Believe me, I'm not. If Blaise can take something that's mine, he will. And you're mine, Shannon—don't ever forget that.'

'Rick, I'm not engaged to you any more——'

As though she hadn't spoken, he repeated heavily, 'You're mine.'

Her palm was slippery with sweat where it gripped the receiver, and she was suddenly, irrationally, very frightened. As much to reassure herself as to convince him, she snapped, 'You're making a fuss over nothing.'

'I don't think so. You don't know Blaise as I do.'

There was another silence, and ridiculously all Shannon could think of was how much this was costing him per minute. 'I'd better go,' he said abruptly. 'I'm supposed to be meeting a couple of people at the bar before dinner—Gerald Thurston's one of them—you met him, remember? I don't expect I'll be able to get away from here before the end of the week.' He paused. 'Look, I'm sorry if I've been sounding a bit paranoid about Blaise—but as I keep saying, I have reason to be. If I didn't love you, Shannon, I wouldn't care where he was or what he did. But I do love you, and I want to marry you, and it scares the hell out of me to think of you being there with him. Do you understand?'

'Well, not really—you seem to be going on the assumption that I'm going to fall into his arms just because he's here.' Fiercely she stifled the image of herself sharing Blaise's bed in the night, of his head lying heavy on her breast.

'Sweetie, I've watched the way women flock around Blaise. I shouldn't think he's ever had one say no to him yet—so I could hardly blame you if he managed to pull the wool over your eyes, too. He's a very smooth operator, is Blaise.'

Knowing she didn't want to hear any more of this and faintly horrified by the intensity of her aversion, Shannon said crisply, 'Thanks for the warning.'

'I had to say it, Shannon. Oh hell, there's Gerald—I've got to go.' His voice deepened attractively. 'Take care of yourself, honey, and remember that I love you. I'll try and call you again tomorrow.'

'Goodbye, Rick,' she said slowly, but the connection had already been cut. She replaced the phone on the hook and for several minutes stood still, lost in thought. Earlier she had sensed she was being drawn into the long-existing conflict between the two men, and this phone call had confirmed all her fears; according to Rick, any interest that Blaise might show in her would be motivated solely by the fact that he thought she belonged to Rick. . . . Was it true? Somehow the tenderness Blaise had shown her in the night, and then his furious reaction towards her this morning, could not be made to fit this theory. Besides, why had he taken so much trouble with her when she was blind—taking her out, talking to her about her mother, insisting she come to the hospital, inviting her to Hardwoods? The end result had been to put her in Rick's path again—and why should he want that? Unable to answer any of her own questions, she rubbed her forehead, conscious of the beginnings of a headache. Getting her book from the library, she went upstairs to her room, and once again it was a relief to close the door behind her and be alone.

CHAPTER EIGHT

WHEN Shannon went down for breakfast the next morning, the first person she saw as she walked into the dining room was Blaise, standing at the buffet pouring himself another cup of coffee. He looked formidably handsome in a pair of lean-fitting grey slacks and an open-necked pale blue shirt; there was colour back in his face, while the early morning sun glinted gold in his thick blond hair. In a leisurely fashion his eyes moved up and down her slim figure; she was wearing a light green flared skirt and a ruffled green and white blouse, her hair pulled back and tied at the nape of her neck with a narrow velvet ribbon.

'Good morning, Shannon,' he said, his expression unreadable.

She smiled nervously. 'Hello.' He moved back to the table with his coffee and she saw that he was limping very slightly. 'Is your leg still sore?'

'A bit,' he said impatiently.

'How are you feeling?'

He hunched his shoulders, stirring his coffee with unnecessary vigour. 'Like a caged animal—if I don't get out of this house today, I'll go crazy.'

With attempted indifference she replied, 'Well, there's no reason why you can't go out, is there?'

'What are you doing today?'

She deliberately turned her back to him, going over

to the buffet to help herself to some crisply fried bacon and fluffy scrambled eggs. 'Goodness, I don't know,' she said lightly. 'It's too early to tell—I'm scarcely awake yet.'

'Why don't we get a lunch packed, and take off for the day—go wherever we please?'

There was no warmth in his voice, and as she walked back to the table she saw his eyes coolly scrutinising her face as he waited for her reply. With a quick spurt of anger she said, 'I don't think you really want my company at all.'

'You're quite wrong.'

'Oh? Then are you one of those people who finds it impossible to crack a smile first thing in the morning?'

He straightened in his chair and Shannon braced herself for whatever might come next. With complete unexpectedness he suddenly grinned at her, his white teeth gleaming, and her heart did a flip-flop in her breast. 'I deserved that,' he said. 'Let's start all over again. Shannon, I'd like you to spend the day with me—will you?'

There was only one possible answer. 'I'd love to.'

'Good! I'll go and ask Stepton to arrange some lunch for us, and I'll see Sam about the car. Meet you outside in—say half an hour?'

She nodded, watching his lean-limbed stride as he left the room. A whole day with Blaise . . . it seemed like a gift. The sunlight striking the crystal vase on the table was splintered into all the hues of the rainbow and she knew a rush of joy as pure and brilliant as the light itself. It was going to be a perfect day, she thought with absolute confidence—just a perfect day.

And so it was at first. They drove farther up the valley, stopping to meander along the side roads, to watch the streams that rolled under the stone bridges, to chat with a couple of farmers. Blaise seemed utterly relaxed, and Shannon could not help contrasting him with Rick, whose frenetic energy and inability to enjoy the peace and solitude of the outdoors world she knew only too well. With Rick there had to be objectives and goals, order and speed. Not for him a quiet walk along a country lane that led nowhere in particular. . . .

They had parked the car by the side of the road, taking the picnic basket with them as they followed the narrow track that led along the banks of a stream. The water, crystal clear and very cold, rolled and splashed around moss-covered rocks, its continuous chatter punctuated by the chirring of blackbirds and the high-pitched peeping of flocks of kinglets. Under the trees the ferns were fresh and green, while scattered in the grass were scarlet wild strawberries, sweet to the taste. Shannon stooped down to pick some, her fingers and lips soon stained red. Collecting some in the palm of her hand, she went over to Blaise, who had been spreading out the blanket in a hollow in the ground where the sun's warmth was trapped. They ate the picnic that the cook had prepared, not talking much, yet with no sense of strain between them; afterwards, Blaise lay back on the grass, resting his head on his rolled-up jacket and grinning lazily at his companion. 'You don't mind if I have a sleep, do you?'

'I think that's a rhetorical question!'

'Quite right.' He yawned and closed his eyes, and within minutes she saw that he had fallen asleep. She could still see in his face the toll of his recent illness, although she knew he would make light of this should she mention it. Sitting cross-legged on the blanket beside him she studied his face, wishing it could reveal to her the answers to all the questions Rick had raised. Strength of character, an imperious will, and an iron control were all to be seen under the merciless glare of the sunlight. Yet she knew only too well how those carved lips, now so firmly held, could be sensual and tender and how the piercing blue eyes could soften and blur with desire . . . not liking her own thoughts, Shannon got to her feet. Moving very quietly so as not to disturb him, she closed the lid of the picnic basket, then wandered through the trees to the brook, beginning to follow its course up the hillside. She watched a squirrel leap from branch to branch of the spreading pines, scolding her as it went; without quite the same pleasure she saw a grass snake slither from its resting place on a sunwarmed boulder into a crevice in the rocks. A little tributary bubbled down the slope to join the brook, and all along its banks were clustered the tiny purple and white faces of wild violets. She knelt down to pick a few, carefully wrapping their stems in the damp moss that covered the rocks. Absorbed in her task, she did not hear Blaise's soft-footed approach; however, instinctively she sensed that she was being watched. She gazed around her, her green skirt and blouse blending into the dappled shadows on the ferns, and her wide eyes reflecting the same hue. She saw him almost immediately, standing by a rough-barked maple whose branches drooped over the brook. 'I didn't hear you coming.'

'I hope I didn't scare you. You looked so beautiful bending over the water that I didn't want to disturb you.'

She flushed. Hastily she got to her feet, holding out the bunch of flowers. 'These are what's beautiful. Look at them, Blaise—the purple veins in the petals. The gold centres, each one perfectly made.' As so often had happened in the last few days, she was suddenly over-whelmed by the sheer miracle of having her sight restored and there was a sheen of tears in her eyes as she looked up at her companion. 'It's because of you that I can see them—I can never thank you enough for that, Blaise.'

It was a shattering of the sylvan peace when he winced

away from her, his eyes suddenly hard. 'I don't want your gratitude.'

The bouquet dropped to her side, her face as shocked as if he had slapped her. 'But of course I'm grateful—how could I not be?'

'Is that why you looked after me when I was ill—because you were grateful? Is that why you got into my bed?' She made an inarticulate gesture, her cheeks scarlet. 'Is that why you're with me now?'

'No!' she burst out. 'I came because I wanted to come. But even if I did come because I was grateful to you—what's wrong with that?'

She might just as well not have spoken. 'You must have spent quite a bit of time with Rick since you got out of hospital—your motive surely can't be gratitude there.'

Shannon said coldly, 'It would have been hard to avoid him, as we were both living in the same house.'

'How very convenient—normally, you know, he hardly ever stays at Hardwoods—it's far too rustic for Rick.'

Although she recognised that what he was saying was almost undoubtedly the truth, all she said was, 'Then perhaps he just wanted to be with me.'

'Yes . . . are you still in love with him?'

Not for anything would she reveal her inner confusion to this hard-eyed stranger, so horrifyingly different from the easy-going companion of this morning. 'Perhaps,' she said coolly, plucking a fern frond from its stem and examining it as if she had never seen one before.

'You'll have to do better than that, Shannon.'

'Why, Blaise?' She met his gaze with deliberate challenge. 'What business is it of yours what I feel about Rick?'

He took a step towards her and she was suddenly acutely aware of the silence of the forest all around them. 'Because I know damn well he wants you back.'

'How can you know that? You haven't even seen him lately?'

'I know the way his mind works.'

The whole conversation was beginning to seem like a crazy mirror image of the one she had had with Rick the night before. She said slowly, 'Why do you hate each other, you two?'

His eyes narrowed. 'I never said I hated him, Shannon.'

'I think you do.'

'Then you're wrong.' Indifferently he added, 'What he feels about me is another question and I'm not prepared to speculate on that. What I do want to know is how *you* feel about him.'

'Blaise, until last week I hadn't seen him for over a year. I'd learned to live without him. It's far too soon for me to know what I feel.'

'I see.' He advanced another step and she stifled the urge to retreat, her fingers unconsciously crushing the fragile stems of the violets. 'Maybe this will help you make up your mind.'

His body loomed over hers, yet there was an exquisite gentleness in his hands as they slid up her arms from her wrists to her shoulders, where he slowly kneaded her flesh. 'Don't look so scared—I won't hurt you. But I've been wanting to do this ever since you walked into the dining room this morning.'

Hypnotised by his gaze, she lost contact with the surrounding forest, the bubble of the stream, and the calling of the birds; there was nothing left but eyes the colour and intensity of the sky, in whose depths she was lost . . . but then his mouth found hers and his arms drew her closer and she shivered with delight, her last rational thought being that at some subconscious level she too had been wanting this all morning. . . .

Restraint melted into desire and desire to passion.

With his lips and hands and body he assaulted all her senses until she ached with the need of him, her fingers clinging to him as though she were drowning, her heart pounding in her breast.

Nothing could have prepared her for what he did next. Suddenly her hands were clutching empty air and there was a space between them and only his hold on her shoulders kept her from falling. Trembling, she stared at him, unable to speak, her dazed green eyes asking the question she could not articulate.

'I want you to do something for me,' he said, each word like a drop of ice-cold water on her over-heated skin. 'The next time Rick kisses you, I want you to remember what just happened between us. If he can arouse you in the same way that I can, well and good—go ahead and marry him. But if he can't—and I'm sure he can't—don't even contemplate living with him, Shannon. In effect you'd be committing suicide, because at an elemental level that's all-important you and he would be lost. Unable to communicate. Cut off from each other. You'd end up in the divorce courts.' He shook her slightly. 'Do you understand what I'm saying?'

Shannon closed her eyes, no longer able to stand his merciless gaze; fighting for breath, she said shakily, 'That was a horrible thing to do—you manipulated me like a puppet!'

'Nonsense, Shannon. It takes two people to create the kind of reaction that happens between you and me.'

She threw caution to the winds. 'Then according to your reasoning, perhaps *you'd* better marry me!'

Blaise traced the vulnerable line of her mouth with one finger, and in spite of herself she swayed towards him, her lips parted. 'Perhaps I should,' he said silkily. 'Except that I don't like poaching on another man's property. Rick has asked you to marry him, hasn't he?'

There was no point in prevarication. 'Yes.'

His eyes gleamed dangerously. 'And what was your answer, little Shannon?'

'No,' she said bluntly, and a second later could not have said if she had imagined the lightning-fast flicker of relief that crossed his face.

'Just like that?'

She glared at him. 'Just like that. I told him it was far too soon and I needed more time.'

'I'm glad you showed at least that much sense.'

'Why don't you want me to marry Rick, Blaise?' she asked. 'What possible difference can it make to you?'

'You'd be throwing yourself away—you're worth ten of Rick.'

'Is that the only reason?'

'If there are any other reasons, my dear, you're not going to hear about them now—you'll have to wait to have your curiosity satisfied.'

'What?' she mocked. 'Blaise Strathern afraid to speak his mind?'

'Discretion in this case is definitely the better part of valour.'

His brilliant eyes bored into hers and with a little shock of surprise, she blurted, 'You're enjoying this, aren't you? This—cat and mouse game.'

He smiled wolfishly. 'But of course. It's been a long time since I've met a woman who can hold her own as well as you can. And who excites me as much as you do.'

She tilted her chin defiantly, his outrageous candour making every nerve end in her body quiver into life. 'Am I supposed to feel flattered by that?'

'Indeed you are,' he drawled. 'I've known a fair number of women in my life.'

'Rick insinuated as much.'

'I'm sure he did. Perhaps what he neglected to say was that sooner or later each and every one of them ended up boring me.'

Provocatively she smiled up at him. 'Do I bore you, Blaise?'

In a scrutiny as leisurely as it was blatantly possessive, he let his eyes wander over her body and again every nerve leaped and she was unashamedly aware of being gloriously, tinglingly alive. 'No, Shannon—you do not in any way bore me.'

A vagrant breeze overhead stirred the branches so that the pattern of sun and shadow shifted on her slender form, making of her an insubstantial creature, unreal and wraithlike. Blaise suddenly reached out a hand and grasped her arm as though to reassure himself that she was indeed flesh and blood, and somehow this action touched her deeply, for it bespoke a need for reassurance underlying his confidence and sophistication; it made him more real than had that devouring, devastating kiss, or the parry and thrust of their conversation. More real, more vulnerable . . . more lovable. The colour drained from her cheeks and her throat closed in panic. No, she thought frantically. No—she didn't love Blaise Strathern. She couldn't . . . yet why she was so afraid, she could not have said.

'What's the matter?'

Although she fought for composure, her reminiscent shudder was all too genuine. 'Someone must have walked over my grave,' she said with an attempt at lightness that did not quite succeed.

She could not tell whether he believed her or not. But the mood of excitement and challenge that had existed between them was gone. The breeze stirred her hair and she shivered, for the first time aware of the shadowed coolness of the forest, of the dampness emanating from the rushing water.

'You're cold,' Blaise said abruptly. 'We'd better go.'

She followed him back to the clearing, and in a con- strained silence they gathered up their things and returned to the car. Shannon leaned back in her seat, feeling very tired and oddly depressed. Apparently equally disinclined to talk, Blaise drove home far more rapidly than he had on the way out, the big car eating up the miles. Even so, it was late afternoon by the time they pulled up by the garage. The limousine was parked there, and Blaise said flatly, 'Looks as though Dad and Louise are back.'

'I thought they weren't coming until tomorrow.'

'So did I.'

There was something undefined in his voice that made her glance at him. She said tentatively, 'They haven't seen you for quite a while—they'll be pleased you're home.'

He shrugged noncommittally. 'Perhaps. Are you coming?'

She had planned to go straight to her room and change before dinner, knowing what a stickler Charles was for punctuality. Instead she heard herself say, 'Of course—I'm anxious to hear if they enjoyed themselves.'

He led her through the front door and the hallway into the living room, its sterile neatness making Shannon aware of her disordered hair and of the grass stains on her skirt. Louise, exquisitely groomed as always, was standing by the window smoking a cigarette in a long gold holder. She heard them coming and turned to greet them, a strange satisfaction in her catlike eyes as she surveyed the couple in the doorway. Her dinner dress, this time of smoke-grey crêpe, swayed gracefully as she walked towards them. 'Darlings,' she said, 'how nice to see you both. How well you're looking, Shannon—Blaise's company must be good for you. And Blaise—lovely to have you home again.'

She held out one beringed hand, and with a smile that held both mockery and affection, Blaise raised it to his lips. 'Hello, Louise. You get more beautiful all the time.'

'Flatterer!' Louise laughed, obviously delighted. 'Get Shannon a drink, darling, and pour one for yourself. What have you been up to, Shannon, since we went away? Isn't it fortunate that Blaise turned up just when you were alone and needing company?'

Shannon was astute enough to interpret this otherwise: Louise, possessive as a she-cat as far as her younger son was concerned, would be only too pleased to see Shannon involved with Blaise rather than Rick. 'Wasn't it?' she smiled, unable to prevent herself from adding airily, 'When Rick phoned me last night, I was able to tell him I was in good hands.'

The sleepy grey eyes flickered. 'Did he say when he'd be back?'

'Not before the end of the week. He seemed pleased with the way things were going. Oh, thank you, Blaise,' as she accepted a sherry from him.

'I see,' said Louise thoughtfully. She glanced at her watch, a sliver of platinum and diamonds on her wrist, 'The Thurstons—you met them, Shannon—are joining us for dinner at eight. Gerald may have more up-to-date news of Rick, as he's just flown back from Vancouver.'

'I'd better go and get changed, then,' said Shannon in faint alarm, not wanting to meet Joan Thurston in her present dishevelled state.

Deliberately Blaise intervened in the conversation. 'You look very beautiful as you are.' She glanced up at him, her cheeks tinged with colour, and just as deliberately he brushed a strand of hair back from her face, his touch a lingering, blatant caress.

The voice that spoke from the doorway cut like a whip. 'Shannon is a guest in our house, Blaise—kindly keep your hands to yourself while she's here.'

There was a deadly silence. Then Charles strode across the rug and two pairs of ice-blue eyes clashed and held. 'Hello, Dad,' Blaise said very quietly, and Shannon felt her fingers tighten around the stem of her glass. 'Welcome home.' He raised his glass in a mocking salute. 'Aren't you going to reciprocate?'

'Of course I'm glad you're back,' said Charles with patent insincerity, his manner as austere as his severely tailored evening wear.

With the smoothness that Shannon could only presume came from long practice, Louise interposed, 'Charles darling, get me another drink, would you? Blaise, was it a worthwhile trip? Did you accomplish what you wanted to?'

'Oh, yes. I got the place set up. There was a hell of a lot of administration, unfortunately, so I never did get involved in the actual dig. I'll probably take a trip up there later in the summer to see how things are going—there should be some extremely interesting developments if all goes well.' He could not prevent the enthusiasm that crept into his voice and Shannon smiled inwardly; she too had experienced that all-encompassing fascination that the past could have. About to ask a question, she heard Charles speak first.

'Have you seen Rick since you got back?'

'No—he'd already gone to Vancouver.'

'He's working on some very tricky and important negotiations that could affect the future of our country for some time to come.'

Shannon stood very still. The message was plain: Rick's work was important; Blaise's was not. She said clearly, 'I think any country that neglects the heritage of its past to focus only on technological progress and visions of future wealth does so at its own peril.'

'Hear, hear,' Blaise said lightly. 'Shannon, it's nearly seven. We'd better go and get changed.' Before she could say anything else, he took her by the arm and steered her out of the room and up the stairs. In the dimly lit hallway outside her door he stopped and she saw that his eyes were brimming with laughter and with some other expression that she couldn't define. 'You can be very fierce when you want to be, can't you?'

She dropped her eyes. 'I shouldn't have said that—your father must think I'm terribly rude. But I was angry.'

'I could see that,' he said quietly. 'You'd be very loyal, wouldn't you, to the man that you loved?'

'I suppose so. If I believed in what he was doing. And I suppose I wouldn't love him if I didn't,' she answered slowly, thinking it out as she went.

He pounced as swiftly as a cat. 'Do you believe in what Rick's doing?'

She stared at him, her eyes appalled. 'No!'

'Why not?'

'It never seems real to me. Or even very honest.'

He nodded with a kind of grim satisfaction. 'Think about what you've just said, Shannon. Think about it very carefully. And now we'd better hurry, or we'll be late for dinner.'

As he strode away from her to go to his own room, she stared after him unseeingly. She did not respect Rick's work: the undercover manoeuvres, the ruthless manipulation of other people's lives, the overriding interest in profit at the expense of the environment.

The inevitable conclusion followed hard on its heels: she did not love Rick. She did not love him at all. What she had been feeling was the ghost of a dead emotion, the last wisps of a love that had been both immature and—her mouth twisted wryly—blind. She had been blind to the real Rick, caught up in a dazzle of romance and parties and fun, seeing only his charm and good looks, flattered by his attention. She had recognised only the superficial, never the real; she had been in love with love.

She swallowed hard, not liking this picture of herself very much, yet knowing it to be the truth. She could never marry Rick now—never. And with this thought came a strange sense of release, for she sensed she had freed herself from a part of the past that might only too easily have caught her in its toils again.

From the landing came the melodious chiming of the old grandfather clock, and she hurriedly abandoned her train of thought before she could begin to contemplate what all this might mean in the future. Blaise was right— she was going to be late if she didn't hurry.

CHAPTER NINE

In half an hour Shannon was ready, and she took another few seconds to give her appearance a quick check in the mirror. She could not help being pleased with what she saw. A hot shower had brought a glow to her skin, while make-up enhanced the brilliance of her eyes and the curve of her mouth, her face framed by the shining brown hair that was loose on her shoulders. She was wearing a white silk blouse, tightly gathered at the cuffs, a plain gold necklace in its plunging neckline; her skirt, slit to the knee, was a severe black. It was an outfit that made her look older and more sophisticated; it was as though she had armoured herself to face Charles's displeasure, the Thurstons' lack of warmth, Louise's lazy sensuality. And what of Blaise? she wondered, gazing at the poised young woman in the mirror. What effect did she hope to have on Blaise?

As if she had conjured him up, there came a tap on her door and his deep voice said, 'Ready, Shannon?'

'Come in.'

The door opened and he stepped inside. In the over-decorated room, so falsely feminine, the girl standing straight and slim by the mirror, made her own statement, without fuss, unafraid.

He stood very still. 'You keep on surprising me,' he said huskily. 'I'm never quite sure how you're going to look, what you're going to say. You fascinate me, Shannon.'

Her heart began to race in her breast and it was an effort to maintain her composure. He, like his father, was wearing conventional evening clothes, although the stark black and white of his impeccably tailored outfit could in no way detract from his male vitality, his startling good looks. 'You look very nice too,' she said inanely.

He came and stood near her so that the mirror reflected their double image. She was wearing high heels, but he still overtopped her by several inches; beside him she looked very slim and fragile. Standing behind her, Blaise brought his hands up to her shoulders and in the mirror their eyes met and held. He slid his hands down her arms to her wrists; he stroked the silky curtain of her hair. Then he caressed the slender line of her throat, following the necklace in its plunge to her breast. And all the while his eyes held hers, mesmerising her. He did not touch her waist, her hips or breasts; he did not kiss her. Yet his slow, deliberate movements, possessive and unhurried, were as openly sexual as any kiss or more intimate caress could have been. Her body knew this, for under his hands it had sprung to life, aching with the desire to feel those hands imprint themselves on every inch of her flesh.

He said quietly, 'I want you—you know that, don't you?'

'Yes.'

'Do you want me?'

Warmth crept into her cheeks, but bravely she held his gaze. 'Yes,' she whispered.

He nodded slowly, as though she had confirmed something he already knew. 'It's a good thing you said no to Rick's proposal.' For the first time since he had entered her room he smiled at her. 'I'll have to make sure you don't have the chance to change your mind, won't I?'

She could think of no reply to this. Her eyes dropped as he turned her to face him. He lowered his head and their lips met. It was as though red-hot coals had burst into flame; consumed by a passionate, pulsing flame, Shannon pulled his head closer, feeling his arms crush her against the lean length of his body. Past and future ceased to exist. There was only the present, and the present was Blaise; he was all she had ever wanted or desired.

It could have been seconds, it could have been minutes before he released her. His lips found the hollow of her throat and under his tongue throbbed all the wildness in her blood. Finally he stepped back and again their eyes met; his were exultant, blazing with a primitive desire for possession, and recognising in hers the equal desire to be possessed. 'I've never wanted a woman as I want you. Some day—or night—very soon, I shall prove that to you.'

Proud as only a woman can be who knows she is desired, she smiled at him, her mouth a soft and sensual curve from his lovemaking. Yet from somewhere deep within her brain there came the first faint stirrings of unease; he wanted her, of that there could be no doubt, yet he had not said one word of love. But then she didn't love him, did she? Remembering how afraid she had felt in the forest, her mind trembled away from the question, and this fear was reflected in the deep green of her eyes.

'Is something wrong?'

'No—no, of course not. Except that we're going to be late.'

'Oh well,' he said philosophically, 'at least now we

won't have to stand around making polite conversation with the Thurstons—not by any means my favourite people.'

Shannon laughed, for she felt very much the same way. Quickly she ran a brush through her hair and re-applied her lipstick, saying sedately, 'Shall we go?'

He offered her his arm, pinpoints of fire still in his eyes, and a few moments later they entered the dining room together. They made a striking couple, he so tall and fair, she dark-haired and slender at his side; tidying her hair and make-up had removed the obvious signs of Blaise's love-making, but colour still glowed in her cheeks, and there was an unconscious intimacy in the quick smile they exchanged as he led her to her seat. Louise's heavy-lidded eyes missed none of this, and she murmured to Gerald Thurston, who was sitting on her right, 'So nice to have Blaise home again—and nice for Shannon to have his company.'

He winked at her roguishly, his voice loud enough that all six of the people now seated around the oval mahogany table could hear him. 'Well, after all, I'm sure Shannon is missing Rick's company—eh, Shannon?'

Very much aware that everyone was staring at her, Shannon said faintly, 'I—of course. But——'

'No buts, young lady,' Gerald continued, the candlelight from the ornate silver candelabrum gleaming on his bald pate. 'Rick told me just yesterday evening that congratulations are in order.'

Blaise was sitting directly across from her and his indrawn hiss of breath sounded shockingly loud. 'For what, Gerald?' he said sharply.

Stepton, his face impassive, was serving paper-thin slices of smoked salmon, and distractedly Shannon murmured her thanks, her fingers clenched in the folds of her starched white serviette as she waited for Gerald's reply. He was waggling his hand playfully and one part of Shannon's brain registered the immense diamond ring wedged on a pudgy finger. 'Now why would we be congratulating a fine young couple like Rick and Shannon?' he said jocularly, taking a large gulp of his wine.

'Get to the point, Gerald,' his wife said waspishly.

'Because wedding bells are going to ring, of course,' Gerald announced. He raised his glass. 'Let's drink a toast to Rick and Shannon, and their future happiness.'

Only Joan and Charles lifted their glasses; Louise was frozen to her chair and Shannon dared not look at Blaise. She licked her lips and said carefully, 'Gerald, I'm afraid there's some mistake——'

'Oh dear, have I let the cat out of the bag?' Gerald said with a show of repentance. 'From the way Rick spoke, I assumed everyone knew.'

'Rick and I are not engaged, Gerald.'

'Well, I know he hasn't put the ring on your finger yet, because he showed it to me—very fine stones, too, young lady. But after all, that's merely a formality, isn't it?'

Feeling as though she was beating her head against the brick wall of Gerald's obstinate personality, Shannon said, 'Rick asked me to marry him before he left, and I said no.' She spared Blaise a quick, desperate glance. 'I told you that, Blaise—remember?'

'Indeed I do,' he said smoothly, and there was no telling from his voice what he was thinking.

'You're being far too coy, my dear,' Gerald said jocosely. 'I might as well tell you I'm delighted by the match—I'd been telling Rick it was time he settled down, and I can't imagine a more beautiful and charming young bride than yourself.' He squeezed a little more lemon juice on his plate. 'Excellent salmon, Charles. Pacific or Atlantic?'

The conversation switched to the relative merits of both fish, and thence to the problems of the fishing industry on the east coast; Louise and Joan were discussing the former's holiday at Thousand Islands. Her head lowered, Shannon struggled to swallow some of the salmon, afraid to even look at Blaise. Surely he wouldn't believe Gerald's story? Surely he would realise that for some reason Rick was pretending to an engagement that did not exist? Then she heard Blaise speak, his voice pitched purposefully lower than the others' so as to be heard only by her. 'After dinner you and I will go for a walk, Shannon.'

For a fleeting second she did look up and into her mind's eye was burned the image of a pair of implacable blue eyes, a hard line of mouth. 'It's all a lie,' she stammered, suddenly terribly afraid.

But he had already turned away and had smoothly engaged Joan Thurston in conversation. Feeling as though she was trapped in some kind of a nightmare, Shannon struggled to cope with what seemed like an unending succession of food, for none of which she had the slightest appetite; and somehow she managed to talk to Louise about, of all things, crocheting, and to Charles and Blaise—her eyes avoiding his—about baroque music. Finally it was over and there was a general move towards the living room. Blaise took Shannon's arm, his fingers with a grip like steel, yet his voice easy and relaxed. 'If you'll excuse us, I promised Shannon some fresh air after dinner. Nice to see you again, Joan and Gerald.'

'Make it short, young fellow,' Gerald said roguishly. 'She's your brother's fiancée, after all.'

Blaise's fingers tightened on her arm and Shannon suppressed a tiny exclamation of pain. 'I'll keep that in mind, Gerald,' he said lightly, and only Shannon sensed the unleashed fury behind his words.

'Did you give Shannon Rick's letter?' Joan asked her husband, her voice with the hint of disdain that always seemed to be present when she addressed her husband.

'Nearly forgot!' Gerald reached into his pocket and brought out a sealed white envelope. 'There you are— he said to be sure and tell you it came with all his love.'

I bet he did, Shannon thought hopelessly, taking the letter. Turning to Blaise, she said, 'I'll go up and get my coat—I won't be a minute.'

'No need,' he said, inexorably steering her towards the door. 'You can put mine around your shoulders—it's not cold out.'

He was right; it was a beautiful night, a three-quarter moon casting dim shadows on the ground, the sky spangled with stars. Stopping in the gold circle of light cast by the front door lights, Blaise said quietly, 'Open the letter, Shannon.'

'I'm in no hurry to open it.'

'What—a letter from your fiancé and you don't want to read it?'

'He's not my fiancé, Blaise—I keep telling you that.'

'You might as well open it—because if you don't, I will.'

He would, too. Angrily she ripped open the envelope, extracting the single sheet of paper. Holding it up to the light, her eyes skimmed the page. Then, before she could replace it in the envelope, Blaise had plucked it from her fingers and was reading it himself. She waited, her lips compressed, remembering the phrases that had leaped out at her . . . 'Dearest Shannon—you'll never know how happy you've made me . . . the shortest engagement on record . . . with all my love . . .'

Damn Rick, she thought furiously. Damn him, any-way. Before Blaise could say anything, she said coldly, 'That letter is pure fiction.'

'Do you expect me to believe that?'

'I really don't care!'

'Keep your voice down—unless you want Gerald and Joan to hear every word you're saying.' He took her elbow and steered her past the garage towards the rose garden. 'You're telling me one thing—he's telling me another.'

'He's playing some kind of a game, Blaise.'

'Why, Shannon?' he said heavily. 'What's he afraid of? He's never even seen us together—why should he be so determined that I get the message that you're not available?'

'He seems to think you're something of a Don Juan,' she said with attempted lightness.

'Oh, for God's sake!'

Somehow this impatient expletive reassured something in her that had been hurt by Rick's mention of Blaise's prowess with women. 'I made it very clear to Rick how much I owed you,' she said. 'That if it had been left up to him, I'd still be sitting in my mother's house, as blind as a bat.'

'That word gratitude again, Shannon?'

'Why do you dislike it so?'

He stared at her, his eyes almost black in the gloom. 'You really have no idea, do you? And at this point, I don't feel like enlightening you.'

Baffled, she gazed up at him, knowing it would be useless to pursue it further. 'Tell me one thing, then—do you believe my story? Or do you believe Rick's?'

'I want to believe yours, Shannon—God knows I do.' He raked his fingers through his thick hair. 'Let's just leave it for now, shall we?'

He had not answered her question directly and in a sense he did not need to—his reluctance was answer enough. He did not believe her. That she should feel anguish twist within her was frightening, for it showed her how highly she valued his good opinion and how greatly she desired his trust. Yet why should it matter to her what he thought of her? He was a stranger, an enigma, no less so now than when she had been blind.

'What are you thinking?' he demanded.

'How little I know you, or understand you,' she sighed with a helpless little shrug of her shoulders.

'You're wrong, Shannon—you know quite a bit about me,' he said, and she sensed that he was testing her in some way. 'You know that I care what happens to you— if I didn't I wouldn't have brought you to Toronto. And you know I find you desirable.'

She was glad that the dim light hid the mounting flush in her cheeks. 'I also know that you don't trust me.'

With a strange gentleness he stroked her cheek and she felt a shivering begin deep within her. 'Trust takes time, Shannon.'

His fingertips traced her cheekbone, the smooth skin of her cheek, the softness of her mouth, and her whole body leaped in response to his touch. He had said he found her desirable; equally she knew how much she wanted him at some primitive, instinctive level. But was that all? She wanted his trust. She wanted his approval. She wanted his love . . . her heart stopped for a minute, then began banging against her ribs so loudly she was sure he would hear it. She wanted his love because—her mind faltered and numbly she forced the thought to its conclusion—because she loved him. She loved Blaise Strathern. His strength and masculinity, his obstinate care of her, his pride and his humour—all had drawn her to him as surely as the moon draws the seas, until this moment when she stood before him knowing she loved him, and would until the day she died.

'Why the hell are you staring at me like that? You look as though you've never seen me before.' She licked her lips, totally at a loss how to answer him. He leaned forward. 'Shannon, are you all right?'

'I—I'm fine,' she stammered, knowing her words were far from the truth. For she loved a man who could not bring himself to trust her; who, though he said he desired her, had never said he loved her. A man whom Rick had warned her against . . . she shivered suddenly, her face pinched and pale.

'You're cold.' Before she could evade him, he drew her towards him; of their own volition her hands slid around the hard arc of his rib cage, and she rested her cheek on his chest, feeling the strong, steady beating of his heart. This was where she wanted to be, she thought in utter wonderment. It was home. It was belonging. Here in his arms was all the security she would ever need, all the joy and all the love.

As though some of her own mood had been communicated to him, he held her quietly for a few minutes, his cheek resting on her hair, his nostrils inhaling its sweet scent. Then, of one accord, they drew apart a little. Her vision had adjusted to the dark now and she could see the grave smile on his lips, the steadiness in his eyes. She smiled back equally gravely, feeling as though something momentous was about to happen. 'Beautiful Shannon,' he said softly. His kiss was slow and sure, all the passion of which she knew him to be capable somehow in check, as though he wanted through his lips to tell her something very different.

They separated and she gazed at him wordlessly, unable to define just what had happened between them. An unspoken commitment? A promise of something to come? At the moment it did not even seem to matter, for she was filled with a vast contentment.

'We'd better go in—we don't want to give Gerald any of the wrong ideas,' he said finally, his words holding no rancour.

Was he beginning to trust her? Her eyes searched his face and she knew it must be so. She tucked her hand in his sleeve. 'All right.'

The rest of the evening passed uneventfully, and when Shannon went to her room, nothing had occurred to mar the peace and happiness which had enfolded her as surely as Blaise's arms. A change had occured in their relationship, she knew; although she had no idea where it would lead, she was content to wait and see, trusting in Blaise as, hopefully, he would come to trust in her. When she got into bed, sleep came almost immediately, a deep and refreshing sleep, dreamless and relaxed.

She awoke to the gentle patter of rain on the roof. Stretching with a lazy sensuality, she padded over to the window and looked out. Grey mist blurred the hills and fields; the river was a grey ribbon carelessly flung on a vivid green backdrop. Shannon had always loved walking in the rain and now she found herself wondering if today she and Blaise would go for a walk hand in hand along the river's edge, talking, sharing their thoughts, learning more about each other. And perhaps, just perhaps . . . unconsciously her lips curved in a smile, her green eyes far away and full of dreams.

She dressed with care in a flared grey skirt and a figured chiffon blouse—very feminine clothes, that she was honest enough to admit she was wearing with Blaise in mind. However, when she went down to the dining room, she was the only person there. She grimaced, acknowledging how ridiculous it was to expect Blaise to be there simply because she wanted him to be. She was helping herself to grapefruit when Stepton came in carrying a highly polished silver coffeepot. 'Freshly made, Miss Shannon,' he said with the slight lifting of the lips that for him passed as a smile.

Because she was still buoyed up by the conviction that something wonderful was going to happen, she beamed at him. 'Good morning—and thanks, I'd love a cup. Where's everybody else?'

'Madame will be down later,' Stepton said diplomatically. 'Mr Strathern has gone to town for the day, and Mr Blaise has already eaten.'

'Oh.'

Only a monosyllable, but Stepton must have caught the faint echo of disappointment in her voice. 'The morning mail delivery brought him a number of reports he'd apparently been waiting for. He said he'd be working in his room most of the day.'

'I see.' Shannon stirred a spoonful of sugar into her coffee, knowing this was just the opportunity she had been waiting for; subconsciously she had wanted the opportunity to speak to Stepton, who she had sensed some time ago was aligned with Blaise rather than with Charles. Taking her courage into her hands, she said, 'Stepton, this is really none of my business, but I can't help noticing that Blaise and his father don't get along very well. Rick told me once that Blaise left home at sixteen and that his father never forgave him—is that the only reason?'

Extracting a square of linen from his pocket, Stepton reflectively rubbed at an imaginary spot on one of the silver trays on the counter. 'No, miss, that's not the reason . . . not really. It all goes back a long way.'

'Yes?' she murmured encouragingly.

Still absently polishing the tray, his faded grey eyes focussing somewhere out of the window, Stepton said slowly, 'The first Mrs Strathern, whose name was Ghislaine, was the most beautiful lady I ever saw in my life—so young and so alive—and so much in love with Mr Charles, and he with her, that it almost hurt to see them together. Even after Blaise was born, they were inseparable. Don't get me wrong—they loved their son as an extension of themselves. But they didn't . . . need him, if you know what I mean. They were entirely self sufficient without him. Maybe as he grew older that would have hurt him almost as much as what did happen . . . who's to know?'

Stepton was so obviously lost in the past that Shannon

knew there was nothing she could do to hurry him. She sat quietly, envisaging in her mind a very different Charles from the cold, austere man she knew: a younger Charles, vibrant and laughing, deeply in love with his beautiful wife Ghislaine, and because of the strength of that love, frighteningly vulnerable.

'On Blaise's fifth birthday they'd planned a surprise for him; they'd bought tickets for a famous circus that was in town, and they were to have dinner together first at a new restaurant that had just opened up. They set off about four o'clock.' Fiercely he rubbed at the tray, holding it up to the light to inspect its shining surface. 'Two hours later we got the message that there'd been an accident. Blaise's mother was dead and his father seriously hurt. Blaise escaped with only minor scratches and bruises, and we all thought how lucky he'd been. Little did we know. . . .'

Shannon could keep silent no longer. 'Know what, Stepton?'

He looked straight at her, the ghost of an old pain in his voice. 'We found out later from Mr Charles exactly what had happened. The car that had caused the accident failed to stop at a red light. The driver was drunk. Mr Charles tried his best to avoid him, but couldn't. When she saw what was going to happen, Madame could perhaps have saved herself. But she chose not to, and instead she threw herself across her son to protect him from the impact. She was killed instantly, while Blaise, as I said, escaped uninjured. Mr Charles has never been able to forgive Blaise for being the one who was left alive.'

'But, Stepton, that's a terrible thing to say!'

'Terrible or not, miss, it's the truth. For a long time Mr Charles couldn't bear to even see Blaise, so the boy was packed off to a series of boarding schools. He'd get himself expelled from one and come home, only to be sent off to another. After a while he stopped trying to come home. Then Mr Charles married the second Mrs Strathern and Master Rick was born and we all hoped things would smooth over. I suppose to a certain extent they did—at least Blaise could come home now on holidays. He was genuinely pleased to have a new brother and made a real effort to be friends with the boy. Maybe he hoped that would mend the rift between himself and his father. But it never worked. . . .' Stepton's brow puckered in thought. 'Perhaps unconsciously Mr Charles poisoned the younger boy's mind against his brother. Well, for whatever the reason, Master Rick always resented his brother, and after a time Blaise stopped making himself available. He went to school; in his free time he wandered the woods and fields; on weekends he stayed as often as possible with friends. And on his sixteenth birthday, the day he was legally of age to leave home, he did just that—left for school in the morning and didn't come back.'

'Whatever did he do?' Shannon asked.

'Got a job on a cargo ship. Jumped ship at Johannesburg and worked his way up through Africa, the Middle East, Greece and Europe. Three years later he came back to Canada, enrolled at university and eventually got his Ph.D. He's the top man in the country in his profession by now, and his reputation's worldwide. But to this day he rarely comes to Hardwoods, and all the old enmity and bitterness still lie between him and his father.'

'I know just what you mean,' Shannon said hopelessly. 'Is there nothing can be done?'

'The second Mrs Strathern, in all fairness, and despite the fact that she dotes on Master Rick, has tried to make Blaise feel more welcome here, and to a limited extent she has succeeded. But—and I hate to sound pessimistic —I think it all goes too deep to ever be truly healed.'

'It seems such a waste. . . .'

In the hallway the telephone began to ring. The imperturbable butler's mask dropped over Stepton's face, and he said as formally as if the preceding conversation had never occurred, 'Excuse me, miss.'

Left alone, and with her appetite quite gone, Shannon went to stand by the window, where the rain dripped from the eaves. At the age of five Blaise had lost both parents: his mother by death, his father by a hatred his child's mind could not even have begun to understand. Stepton had glossed over the next eleven years, but Shannon could imagine all too well the bewilderment, the fear, and the loneliness that must have dogged every footstep the young boy had taken. At sixteen he had made the leap to adulthood and had struck out on his own . . . but in effect he had been on his own for years. And this was the boy who had grown up into the man upstairs, who had hounded her out of her self-pity and isolation, who had freed her from Lorna's possessiveness, who had given her back her sight. The man whose kisses stirred her blood, whose caresses aroused in her longings she had not known existed. . . .

CHAPTER TEN

UNABLE to stay still, Shannon left the dining room and ran upstairs. The end door in the corridor was closed and from within came only silence. Grabbing a raincoat and boots, she went outside and walked until lunchtime, a meal she shared with Louise, who was irritatingly at her most indolent. Afterwards she read for a while. She wrote letters to her mother and to Bridget. She mended a blouse. She knew there was no use in seeking out Sam's companionship, for he was in town with Charles; Stepton at lunchtime had been so frostily formal that she could only assume he was regretting his confidences; and Blaise, the only one she really wanted to see, was still shut in his room. As she sat on her bed, she heard footsteps coming up the stairs and, embarrassed to be found so obviously at loose ends, walked out into the hall. It was Peggy, carrying a tea tray.

'I've brought this for Mr Strathern, Miss Hart. Would you like one too?'

'Oh, no, thanks, Peggy.' In quiet decision she said, 'Here, let me take it to him, will you?'

The girl relinquished the tray and Shannon walked down to the end of the hall, balancing it carefully as she tapped on the door.

'Come in!' Blaise called impatiently.

Taking a deep breath, Shannon walked in. Then her eyes widened. The bed and most of the floor were covered with neat stacks of paper. The desk was a litter of maps and typewritten sheets. The wastebasket was overflowing. 'What on earth are you doing?' she blurted.

'All the preliminary reports came this morning from my last project. I have to complete statistics and abridge the whole thing to manageable proportions.' He raked his fingers through his thatch of blond hair. 'I'll be here a week at the rate I'm going.'

'Can I help?' The words were out before she gave herself time to think.

He got up and stretched, the muscles rippling under his shirt. Taking the tray from her, he looked around for somewhere to put it and suddenly they were both laughing as they surveyed the chaos in the room.

'It's not as bad as it looks,' he said defensively. 'At least I know where everything is.'

She giggled and said incautiously, 'You certainly won't be able to sleep in your bed tonight!'

His eyes caught fire, impaling her on sparks of blue. 'Where would you suggest I sleep, then, Shannon?'

Red hot colour burned her cheeks. 'I have no idea,' she stammered.

He put the tray down on top of the typewriter case and walked over to her, unhurriedly surveying her from head to foot. 'No idea?' he repeated softly.

She could not have moved if she had had to. 'Blaise, please——'

Perhaps her wide-eyed confusion touched him. Or perhaps he merely lost interest. At any rate, he turned away, scarcely bothering to conceal his irritation when he spoke. 'You arouse the worst in me, Shannon. You'd better go—I've got a hell of a lot of work to do.'

She hesitated momentarily, knowing the best thing to do would be to leave as he had suggested. 'I asked if I could help.'

'Do you really mean that?'

'I wouldn't have said it if I hadn't.'

It was his turn to hesitate. 'I warn you—I'm a hard taskmaster.'

Demurely she replied, 'That doesn't surprise me.' Suddenly serious, she added, 'But you always drive yourself harder than anyone else.'

He glanced at her sharply and she knew her point had struck home. But all he said was, 'Can you type?' She nodded. 'Okay—we'll get Stepton to bring up another desk. Then if you could type these work sheets in rough copy, I'll revise them so they can be re-typed for the final report.'

At first the work went slowly for Shannon, because Blaise's angular, very masculine handwriting was not particularly easy to decipher and a lot of the vocabulary was highly technical. But she persevered, and two hours later Blaise had to speak to her twice to get her attention. 'Dinner, Shannon.'

'First let me finish this sentence . . . there. That's another page done.'

He picked it up and read it through quickly. 'That's excellent. You're hired!'

She laughed, pushing back a strand of hair and looking at her ink-smudged fingers ruefully. 'I'd better go and clean up. I'll meet you downstairs.'

'Do you feel up to doing a bit more this evening?'

'Sure—I'd like to finish that first section.'

'Why are you helping me like this, Shannon?' he asked abruptly.

'I enjoy it—it's a challenge,' she said honestly.

'I see.'

Feeling that her answer had in some way disappointed him, she watched as he turned away, beginning to unbutton his cuffs. About to leave the room, she saw on the bureau the silver-framed photograph that had caught her attention the night Blaise had been so ill, and heard herself say, 'That photo—is she your mother?'

'Yes—she's been dead since I was five,' he said in a clipped voice.

'I know. Stepton told me all about it—the accident, and how your father hated you afterwards and sent you off to boarding school.'

He turned to face her again; he had been undoing the front of his shirt and his fingers rested on the last button. 'Stepton talks too much.'

'It sounds silly to say I'm sorry—but I am.'

His eyes were as hard as stones. 'Keep your sympathy.'

She had started this and somehow she had to finish it. 'Perhaps it was because of your own problems with your father that you were able to help me with my mother?'

'If you want to believe that, then by all means do so.' Blaise shrugged out of his shirt, and added with heavy patience, 'I'm getting changed, Shannon—unless you want to be embarrassed, I'd suggest you leave.'

'The message being that you don't want to discuss your mother or your father or anything to do with them.'

'Exactly.'

'Shove it all under the carpet and pretend it never happened,' she said recklessly.

'What else am I supposed to do, Shannon? Go and put my arms around my father and tell him I love him—is that what you'd recommend?' His eyes were brilliant with temper.

'Why not? You never know—it might work.'

'The last time I ever did that I was ten years old. He pushed me away and the next day I was sent off on a long visit to some relatives. I vowed then never to do it again—and I see no reason to alter that vow.'

Her own temper died away. In her mind's eye she could see that ten-year-old boy all too clearly; across the years she could empathise with the pain and rejection he must have felt. 'I—I'm sorry, Blaise,' she muttered, staring at his bare chest because she did not want to meet his gaze, her eyes swimming with tears. 'I shouldn't have said that to you—about your father, I mean. It's really none of my business.'

'No, it isn't, is it?' He raised her chin, his eyes intent on the tears trembling on her lashes. 'So why are you so upset?'

She gazed at him in troubled silence. She loved him—that was why . . . and because of that love, she cared about the boy he had been and the man he had become.

He was standing so close that she could see tiny flecks in the blue of his irises; his lashes were as thick as a girl's, and she felt her heart turn over in her breast with love of him. She had been blind in more ways than one, she thought wryly. Weeks ago when he had kissed her in the garden at the restaurant, the truth had been staring her in the face and she had ignored it, in her confusion imagining herself still in love with Rick. Blind indeed, when this man in front of her was all she had ever wanted or would ever need. . . . 'We're going to be late for dinner,' she said huskily.

He suddenly crushed her to his chest, his hand buried in her hair. 'When you look at me like that, all I want to do is hold you and never let you go.'

Her cheek was against his bare shoulder; his skin smelled clean and indefinably masculine. The piercing joy that had followed his words was so intense that she could only cling to him wordlessly.

Along the hallway reverberated the sonorous boom of the dinner gong. There was a thread of laughter in Blaise's voice as he said, 'Saved by the bell—tell Louise I'll be down in a couple of minutes.'

In her own room Shannon quickly applied lipstick and brushed her hair, her mind full of conjectures. She had never met a man so full of contradictions as Blaise Strathern; tender and loving one minute, harsh and angry the next. Yet as she remembered how he had held her only a few minutes ago, saying he never wanted to let her go, the wild hope suffused her that maybe—just maybe—he might come to love her. . . .

The next two days could only strengthen what at first had seemed an irrational dream. She and Blaise worked together in his room and the more she read of the documents, the more intrigued Shannon became. Her questions became more frequent and incisive and often the two of them stopped altogether as Blaise discussed a point that had puzzled her. She worked hard yet with increasing enjoyment, and the rapport between them grew by the hour. Their silences were comfortable; their discussions animated. It was a kind of companionship new to Shannon, who had never been able to share in Rick's interests, and she gradually became aware of an extra dimension to the love she had for Blaise: a meeting of minds, a sharing of a common goal.

She was finishing up some proofreading before dinner on the second day when Blaise walked over to see how she was doing; he leaned over the back of her chair with his arm around her shoulders as she pointed out an error, her face alight with laughter as she glanced up at him.

To the man who, without warning, pushed open the door, it must have seemed an intimate scene: the two heads, one so fair, one so dark, bent over the papers, the voices a low intimate murmur, the man's body curved over the woman's in an attitude at once protective and possessive. The watcher drew in his breath sharply. 'Shannon, what the hell are you doing in here?' he demanded.

Both heads swung round. 'Rick!' the girl exclaimed, smiling at him. 'I didn't know you were coming back today.'

'I'm sure you didn't,' he said unpleasantly, 'or I wouldn't have caught you in Blaise's bedroom.'

She stood up slowly, very much aware of Blaise behind her, his big body utterly still. She said clearly, 'I've been helping Blaise with some reports.' She indicated the piled up papers with one hand. 'As you can see.'

'I can see a great deal,' Rick snarled. 'Although, Blaise, I hadn't thought you'd reached the stage of needing excuses like that to get a woman into your room.'

'Careful, Rick,' Blaise said very quietly.

'Careful, hell!' Rick exploded. 'I come back from a week-long business trip and I find that my fiancée has been closeted in my brother's bedroom for the best part of three days—how am I supposed to feel about that?'

'Nothing has happened here that couldn't have happened in the living room in full view of your parents,' Shannon sputtered furiously. 'And I am *not* your fiancée!'

He flinched as if she had struck him. 'Shannon, you told me the night before I went away that you'd marry me—you can't have forgotten that!'

Fear brushed her, for he looked so genuinely stricken. 'I told you I needed more time—I certainly didn't promise to marry you,' she said steadily. Behind her Blaise shifted position.

'Sweetheart,' Rick said in obvious bewilderment, 'I don't understand what's going on. If this is some kind of joke, I don't think it's very funny.'

'I'm about as far from joking as I could be,' she said stonily.

He reached in his pocket, taking out a velvet-covered jeweller's box. 'Look, I even got you the kind of ring you wanted—remember you asked for a square-cut diamond?' He opened the box and the light flashed cold and pure on the stone's facets.

Shannon swallowed. Sensitive as she was to Blaise's every mood, she was sure he was holding himself in check with great difficulty, and she was terrified of what he might say or do. Somehow she had to convince him that this was some kind of nightmarish game Rick was playing. 'I didn't ask you for a ring, Rick, I didn't say I'd marry you, and I have not been your fiancée for over a year. Furthermore, I——'

'Come off it, Shannon,' Rick cut in. 'Why do you think I told Gerald and Joan we were engaged if we're not? I'm not likely to make a fool of myself in front of my boss, of all people.'

She was momentarily speechless, for his words had the ring of truth about them—Rick cared too greatly about his social position in the business world to jeopardise himself by a foolish and pointless lie. Her uncertainty did not escape Rick. He came closer and took her by the arm, all his charm in his smile. 'You haven't even welcomed me home,' he said softly, and bent his head, his arms unexpectedly strong as they pulled her closer, one hand clamped around her neck as his mouth seized hers.

Rigid with protest, she endured his brief kiss, as well

as the triumph in his pale eyes as he raised his head. 'That's better.' He glanced over at Blaise apologetically, and then back to Shannon. 'Honey, Blaise isn't interested in what's going on between us, and this hardly seems the place to be discussing matters private to us. Let's go downstairs—the library will be empty and we can talk there.' He smiled at her coaxingly. 'I love you too much to want any misunderstandings between us.'

His hand was still tight around her arm and she sensed a watchfulness behind the facile smile. She hesitated irresolutely, wondering if perhaps it wouldn't be better to go with him and lay down a few ultimatums in private; she could talk to Blaise afterwards.

From behind her Blaise said harshly, 'Make up your mind, Shannon—I've got another hour's work to do before dinner, so you can either stay and help me, or else go and have a heart-to-heart talk with your supposed fiancé. One or the other.'

She turned to look at him. His eyes were hooded, inscrutable; his mouth a thin line. It was impossible to tell what he was thinking. 'Which do you want me to do?'

'My dear, don't expect me to make up your mind for you.'

She flushed at the edge in his voice, her decision made. No good would come out of continuing this triangle; she would deal with Rick first, and then get back to Blaise. But first she said, holding the masked blue eyes with her own desperately sincere gaze, 'Blaise, I'm telling the truth when I say I'm not engaged to Rick.'

From Blaise no reaction to her words, only a quick sideways glance at the pile of papers and maps on the desk. Her heart sank. Perhaps Rick was right and Blaise really wasn't interested in whether or not she was engaged; perhaps he didn't care, and all he wanted was to be left alone to get back to work undisturbed. Confused and frustrated, she said brusquely to Rick, 'Let's go downstairs and get this over with,' and without waiting for his response stalked out of the room, her head held high.

The library was empty. As soon as Rick had closed the door behind him, Shannon turned on him like a virago. 'You've got to stop this nonsense, Rick. You know as well as I do that I never promised to marry you.'

With lazy grace he lit a cigarette and blew a cloud of smoke in the air. 'Of course.'

His effrontery made her gasp. 'Then what are you up to?'

'I'm a dog in the manger, Shannon. If I can't have you, then I'm going to make damn sure Blaise doesn't get you either.'

'Blaise has not shown the slightest interest in marrying me!'

'Who are you trying to kid?'

'No one!'

'Come off it, Shannon—I've seen Blaise with a lot of women, and I've never seen him look at one the way he looks at you.'

For a moment she forgot all other considerations but this one statement. 'What do you mean?'

Irritably Rick drew on the cigarette. 'If you don't know, I'm not about to tell you.'

'Why do you hate him so?' she whispered.

For once he looked at her without artifice, his eyes cold and merciless. 'Since I was very young, I've always known that Blaise aroused far stronger emotions in my father than I ever could. I was always accepted and loved—sure. But I could never wake anything like the intensity of feeling that Blaise could; that it was bad feeling is almost irrelevant.'

'That's twisted and horrible,' Shannon protested in distress. 'Blaise had a terrible childhood—how can you add to it?'

'You're very sweet and naïve, Shannon. But, you know, you'd be better off marrying me than Blaise. I'd let you go your own way and I wouldn't ask too much of you—Blaise would devour you. He'd want all of you, body and soul.'

If only he did, the girl thought longingly, unaware of how vividly her face reflected that longing.

'You'd like that, wouldn't you?' Rick said. 'Well, you're not going to get it.'

'If Blaise should decide he wants to marry me, there's nothing you can do about it, Rick—we're two adults, after all,' she answered with as much dignity as she could muster.

'We'll have to wait and see, won't we? And in the meantime,' he consulted his watch, 'we'd both better get ready for dinner. Mother mentioned something about guests.'

At least she could speak to Blaise then, Shannon thought swiftly. 'Very well. And listen, Rick—no more announcements about our engagement.'

'I rarely do the same thing twice in a row,' he said blandly, and with that she had to be satisfied. She ran upstairs and down the hallway, not even stopping at her own room. But when she tapped on Blaise's door, there was no answer. She waited and knocked again. Silence. Carefully she opened the door and looked in. There was no sign of Blaise and his jacket was gone from the back of the chair.

Shannon fought back an acute disappointment that was mingled with uneasiness, knowing she would not feel comfortable until she could tell him what had transpired in the library. She bit her lip in frustration, wondering if she should leave him a note, but deciding against it; she would see him at dinner, after all. With this in mind, she chose a soft clinging dress of silk jersey in a subtle shade of rose, with chunky gold jewellery and gold sandals. Just the thought of seeing Blaise again was enough to bring a wild-rose colour to her cheeks and a sparkle to her eyes, and Rick's manoeuvres suddenly seemed childish and unimportant.

About to leave the room, she heard a tap on her door, and it was as though her thoughts had conjured him up. Sure it would be Blaise, she opened the door. 'Oh,' she murmured, 'Stepton . . . I'm not late, am I?'

'Oh, no, miss. Your mother is on the phone.'

'Thank you—the hall phone?'

Shannon ran lightly downstairs. Lorna had been going through a period of adjustment herself since Shannon had left home, and there was both an uncertainty and a new warmth in their relationship; they had exchanged a number of telephone calls, during which Lorna had been less ready to make demands, more apt to listen. Shannon picked up the receiver. 'Hello, Mother. Nice to hear from you,' she said with genuine feeling in her voice.

'Hello, Shannon. How are you?'

They discussed Shannon's health and Lorna's latest bridge games, and Shannon told her mother about the work she had been doing for Blaise. Then there was a silence, and across the hundreds of miles that separated them Shannon divined a hesitancy in Lorna that intrigued her. 'Is something bothering you?' she asked. 'You sound—different.'

'Well, I——' Lorna hesitated, then started again, some of the old snap back in her voice. 'The truth of the matter is, Shannon, that Harry—Colonel Fawcett to you, dear— has asked me to marry him. And,' with faint defiance, 'I've said yes.'

'Mother! I'm delighted—congratulations! He'll make you very happy.' And he would, for he was just deaf enough that he would not hear all Lorna's comments, and just enough of an old soldier that he wouldn't hesitate to give his wife the occasional order—which was exactly what she needed. 'You should have told me the minute you got on the phone.'

'I was afraid you might not like it.'

'Why ever not?'

'Well, at my age. . . .'

'Nonsense,' Shannon said stoutly. 'You're a very attractive woman and you've been alone a long time.'

Incredibly Lorna sounded almost shy. 'That's just what Harry says. He wanted me to say hello to you, and to assure you you'll always be welcome to come and see us.'

'Thank him for me, won't you? When is the wedding?'

'In three weeks. Will you be able to come?'

'Yes, of course. I'll have had my check-up by then, so I'll be able to fly out. I'll look forward to it, Mother.'

'Now what about yourself?' Lorna demanded. 'Have you and Rick patched things up?'

'No!'

'You sound very sure about that, anyway,' Lorna commented drily.

'Mother——' Shannon hesitated, then took the plunge. 'Rick told me he broke our engagement because you told him to—is that true?'

'Oh, no,' Lorna replied in faint surprise. 'He phoned me and told me he wanted to end it. I have to admit I didn't discourage him, mind you.'

'Then he lied to me,' Shannon said slowly. 'I wouldn't marry him now if he was the last man on earth.'

'Does his brother hold more of an attraction?' Lorna asked slyly. Shannon's hesitation was answer enough. 'Let me tell you something, Shannon,' Lorna said briskly. 'The reason I agreed to your engagement to Rick in the first place is because I knew he'd be easily manageable. I didn't see very much of Blaise, but my impression was definitely not of a man one could wrap around one's finger. He'd be a lot more difficult to live with than Rick—but you'd have twice the man. And now I'm going to stop giving motherly advice and get off the telephone before I end up in the poorhouse. Let me know when your flight will be and we'll meet you at the airport.'

'Lovely! Give my best to Colonel—to Harry, and tell him I'm delighted with your news.'

'Thank you, dear. Take care of yourself. Goodbye.'

''Bye!'

Shannon replaced the receiver and stood for a moment lost in thought. This new development in Lorna's life might never have come about if she, Shannon, had not left home under Blaise's wing, nor would this new closeness have flourished between mother and daughter—a closeness that paradoxically had sprung from their being apart.

She could share the news of her mother's impending marriage with Blaise, she thought, pleased; it would give her the perfect excuse to seek him out. But when she went into the living room it was to find that Rick's report of guests had been only too true; twenty or more people were gathered there and Blaise was at the far side of the room engaged in an animated discussion with a stylishly dressed young couple and a strikingly beautiful redhaired woman in a slim black sheath that shrieked of money. Before Shannon could do more than take this in, Rick was guiding her over to a group of half a dozen people whose names she never did get straight, and when eventually they went in for dinner, whether by accident or design, she and Blaise were seated at opposite ends of the table. However, Shannon was not Lorna's daughter for nothing; she went through all the correct motions, keeping up her end of the conversation, and even, to her private amazement, making the occasional joke. But inwardly she admitted to herself that the long-drawn-out meal was a subtle form of torture; she could see Blaise, she could hear his voice and his laughter, but communication between them was as impossible as if he'd been in another country.

After dinner everyone moved back into the living room, where Shannon was cornered by the Thurstons, unable to escape short of outright rudeness. Then one of the guests played two or three piano selections and under cover of the polite applause, Shannon began to edge her way around the room. But Charles insisted on introducing her to a tall, grey-haired man who was an ophthalmologist and who wanted to hear every detail of Shannon's recovery; from the corner of her eye she saw Blaise and the redhead leave the room together. Somehow, through a haze of mingled hurt and an emotion she recognised quite clearly as jealousy, she managed to keep talking, and if her manner was overly vivacious and her voice a little strained, no one seemed to notice. Finally the other guests started to depart; she went through the round of necessary farewells, saw that Rick was involved in conversation with Gerald and Joan, and thankfully made her escape to her room.

It was a relief to be alone. Her shoulders were aching with tension, her throat was dry, and her eyes stinging from too much cigarette smoke. Hanging up the rose-coloured dress she had put on with such high hopes only a few hours ago, she struggled against a depression that seemed to settle on her like a physical weight, and that stemmed, she knew, from Blaise's avoidance of her. She had needed to talk to him, to clear up the misunderstanding that Rick had precipitated. Yes, she had needed to talk to him . . . but did his behaviour this evening indicate that he felt no similar need? Perhaps he didn't care whether she was still involved with Rick—not enough to make the opportunity to speak with her, anyway.

She creamed her face, her puzzled green eyes gazing at their own reflection. Could that be true? Could it be that Blaise was indifferent to her? She couldn't believe that—she simply couldn't. Not in face of the companionship they had experienced the last few days. The searing, earth-shaking kisses they had shared. He couldn't be indifferent . . . she smoothed away the last of her mascara and brushed her hair. Tomorrow was another day, she thought with rekindled optimism. Tomorrow she wouldn't wait for Blaise to come to her—she would seek him out and tell him exactly what had passed between her and Rick. Knowing Rick as he did, he would surely believe her. . . . She got into bed, not bothering to draw the curtains, and the moonlight splashed gently on the counterpane as she fell asleep.

She did not hear the quiet approach of footsteps along the hall. A hand rested on her doorknob and without a sound the door swung inwards. Momentarily a man's shadow was outlined on the rug. Then it withdrew, leaving the door open, and the footsteps continued their way to the end bedroom, where the watcher seated himself by the window that overlooked the driveway, waiting for the return of a car. It was nearly two hours before his vigil was rewarded. . . .

CHAPTER ELEVEN

SHANNON was dreaming. She must be dreaming, she thought muzzily, for the voice that murmured in her ear was Blaise's and the warm weight beside her on the bed was a man's body. A hand was stroking her bare shoulder and she shivered with delight. Her whispered voice, drugged with sleep, nevertheless sounded loud in the moonlight stillness of the room. 'I'm so glad you're here —I wanted to see you.'

'I know you did.'

Her arm reached up to hold him, for she was afraid that he might vanish. He must be real, for his skin was warm, smooth. Her fingers caressed him lazily; she was cocooned in a delicious lassitude.

From the doorway came a voice harsh and bitter— the same voice that had murmured in her ear only moments ago. Blaise's voice. 'You little bitch! You've been lying to me all along, haven't you?'

Her eyes flew open. Aghast, she saw that the face so close to hers was Rick's. She pushed him away with an inarticulate gasp of horror. 'What are you doing here?'

'I'm here because you invited me, darling.'

'No!' She sat up, totally unaware of the tumble of dark hair across her breast, only knowing the dream had turned to nightmare. Her eyes left Rick, pulled to the all-too-familiar figure of the man in the door. It was Blaise, still in evening clothes: he must just have come home. 'Blaise, I didn't——'

'Spare me, Shannon. I've had all I can take of your protestations of innocence. It's really nothing to me that you choose to sleep with my brother—although it's a pity you couldn't be honest about it and perhaps a little less public.' His eyes dark as midnight, he swept her with a look of such scathing contempt that she quivered as though she had been struck. 'Goodnight.' With exaggerated care, he shut the door.

Scarcely knowing what she was doing, Shannon called out his name, pulling her legs free of the covers. It was Rick's words that brought her to her senses. 'I wouldn't go after him if I were you,' he said lazily. 'When Blaise is as angry as he is now, you never know what he might do.'

She turned to face him. He was leaning on one elbow, naked to the waist, the silver light from the window catching the derisive lift of his eyebrows. Speaking with cold precision, she said, 'You planned this, didn't you? You waited until he came back, so he'd be sure to see us.'

He smiled, a smile that did not reach his eyes. 'I meant every word I said in the library and I figured this little charade would finish anything that might have developed between you and Blaise. It would seem I'm right.'

'I won't let you be right!' she snapped.

'Do you think he'll listen to a word you say now? He has some very puritanical ideas about women, has Blaise —he won't take anyone else's leavings, believe me.'

She pressed her hands against her cheeks, frantically trying to stay calm. 'Blaise is ten times the man you'll ever be, Rick,' she gasped. 'Whatever happens, I'm through with you—I never want to see you again. I think what you've done is despicable. If Blaise and I can't . . .' she stumbled briefly '. . . can't work things out, then I shall leave here tomorrow.' Wearily, she pushed her hair back from her forehead. 'And now get out of my room.'

'Oh yes, I'm going. After all, I've accomplished what I set out to do.' Rick looked her up and down, missing not one detail of her slender, distraught beauty. 'I still think it's a pity you and I didn't stay together.'

'I can't imagine how I ever thought I was in love with you,' she said lifelessly. 'I must have been mad.'

He got up from the bed. 'One last word of advice, Shannon—stay in your room once I've gone. Blaise always was unpredictable, and you might get more than you bargained for if you attempt any kind of a reconciliation at this time of night.' He gave her a mocking salute. 'Goodnight—sleep well.'

She gave him five minutes, during which she sat in frozen stillness on the bed, her hands clenched in her lap. Then she got up, threw her robe around her, and left the room. She had heard Rick's warning and knew he could be right; but stronger than fear was a desperate need to explain to the man she loved why he had seen another man, his own half-brother, in her bed. . . . When she came to Blaise's door, she did not bother knocking. She simply turned the handle and walked in, pulling the door shut behind her.

The room was lit only by the bedside lamp. Blaise was standing by the bed tying the silk cord of a pair of pyjamas trousers; he wore no jacket. His hands grew still when he saw her. His voice without inflection, he said, 'Get out.'

Shannon leaned against the door for support, for one crazy moment wondering what she was doing here. Her voice seemed to have disappeared, so she silently shook her head.

He straightened to his full height. 'I said get out, Shannon.'

'No—not yet. There are things we need to talk about.'

'This is your last chance—get out, or I won't be responsible for what happens.'

Rick, when she had least wanted him to be, had been right—in the mood Blaise was in, he *was* totally unpredictable, as dangerous as a mountain cat. 'Blaise, just give me five minutes, that's all I ask,' she said with the calm of desperation.

'You're not in a position to ask for anything. I can surely credit you with enough intelligence to realise that?'

'Will you just listen to me—please!'

With lazy grace he walked over to her, his eyes never leaving her face. His hand encircled her arm like a steel trap and he began pulling her towards the bed. Unresisting, she allowed herself to be led, although her palms were suddenly damp with sweat. 'You'd better sit down,' he said unpleasantly. 'This could take longer than five minutes.'

She sank down on the end of the bed, hoping he would not notice that her knees were shaking. When he let go of her, she absently rubbed the red mark his fingers had left on her flesh, knowing that he was waiting for her to begin and knowing also that now she had the chance she had been waiting for, her mind had gone completely blank.

'I thought you had something to tell me.' Blaise's eyes wandered insolently over the swell of her breasts under the filmy, lace-edged nightgown. 'Or perhaps it wasn't talk you had in mind?'

'Yes, it was,' she jerked out, instinctively shrinking away from him.

'It wouldn't say much about Rick's prowess as a lover if you immediately had to come to another man's bed, would it?'

His ugly words gave her the impetus she needed. 'Blaise, I know it must have looked as though Rick and I were lovers——'

'Oh yes, it looked all of that,' he interrupted grimly.

Equally grimly, she ploughed on. 'It wasn't what you thought. He admitted in the library that he was playing games with us—and his being in my room was just another example of that.' Blaise's cold-eyed stare was unnerving her, so that her words, instead of sounding convincing, sounded merely placatory. 'You see, I was asleep. He must only have come into my room a few minutes before you got there. And when I woke up...' Realising what she was about to say, she blushed uncomfortably, her lashes fluttering down to hide her expression. '... well, I thought it was you.'

She was totally unprepared for his next move. Swift as an animal, he flung her back on the bed, holding her prisoner by the wrists. 'Do you really expect me to believe that?' he snarled. 'You and Rick were once lovers—don't bother denying that any more—and you're saying you couldn't tell the difference between him and me?'

'I told you—I only just woke up.'

'God! You sicken me.'

In the face of his scalding contempt, Shannon did the only thing possible and lost her temper completely. 'I don't give a damn!' she cried. 'You're not listening to a word I say, are you? No, you've condemned me right from the beginning. What's the matter, Blaise? Because your mother died and left you alone, do you hate all women? Is that it?'

'Leave my mother out of this,' he said with dangerous calm.

'I hit home, didn't I?' Furious, her eyes blazing like emeralds, she tried to fight free of his hands, but all she accomplished was to tear the sleeve of her robe and snap the narrow strap of her nightgown, baring the creamy pale skin of one breast. At the look in his eyes the colour faded from her face and she shrank back against the mattress. 'Don't, Blaise——'

He lowered himself on her, his weight pinioning her to the bed. Then his mouth was tracing the slow rise of her breast to its tip. She fought against the aching sweetness that invaded her, knowing that for him to make love to her now would be the worst possible thing that could happen. Not now, not when he was angry, despising her, believing her to be Rick's mistress. 'Let me go,' she pleaded, her temper gone, her pride in rags.

'Why should I?' he said almost conversationally. 'You came to my room of your own free will.'

'Not for this,' she whispered.

'I warned you you might get more than you bargained for if you stayed.'

And so he had, she recalled wretchedly. 'I only wanted to explain——'

But his mouth came down hard on hers, forcing her lips apart so she could feel his slow, sensuous exploration. Again that aching tide of desire threatened to carry her far from the shores of control and good sense. Again there was a futile struggle to free herself. But the frantic movements of her hips and thighs only caused him to press himself harder against her so that she felt the power and strength of his arousal. It both terrified and excited her. As if he had measured her excitement to the exact degree, he released her wrists, his hands pushing her gown to her waist and stroking the fullness of her breasts, even as his hips moved slowly and sinuously against hers.

Shannon ceased to fight. With one hand buried in his hair, she drank deeper of his kiss; with the other she began a deliberately sensual caressing of his chest, its hard bone and muscle and sinew so different from her own softness. Because she loved him, she could acknowledge to herself how much she wanted him, how she longed both to possess and be possessed, to give him pleasure even as she received it. And across the very back of her mind flashed the quicksilver thought that if he made love to her, he would know without a doubt that she had never been loved by any man before . . . he would know she had been telling him the truth all along.

Lost in a pulsing world of sheer delight, she was vaguely aware that his kiss had gentled; he was nibbling at her lips, his hands still rhythmically stroking her body until she quivered at his touch like the strings of a harp. Her dark hair tangled on the bedspread, she smiled at him with her eyes, her face flushed and languorous with desire. It seemed as if all the barriers were down, for his own eyes were blurred with an answering passion. Everything was all right, she thought, her heart welling with happiness. Tracing the leanness of his cheek with one finger, feeling the roughness of his beard and the carved line of his mouth, she said very softly, 'I love you, Blaise.'

She felt the shock run through his body like an electric charge. He reared up on his elbows and for a moment that afterwards she was sure she must have imagined, she saw a fleeting agony darken his eyes. Then it was gone and in its place an anger so corrosive that she flinched. 'Did you tell Rick you loved *him* an hour ago?'

It was as if he had taken the very best gift she could give him and flung it back in her face. The pain was so intense, so physical, that she almost cried out. Briefly the hard blue eyes were shadowed by uncertainty. 'Shannon?'

She shook her head, knowing herself defeated: she had gambled and lost. The only thing left to do was retreat with as much dignity as possible. Blaise had rolled free of her, pulling her to her feet, and she hugged the flimsy protection of her robe around her. Shamefully she knew she was going to start crying in a minute and that she could not bear for him to see her do so. His hand was still on her arm, restraining her, so she said as composedly as she could, 'Let go, please. I've had enough of this— I want to go to my room.'

The uncertainty was gone. 'That's the most sensible thing you've said yet. And listen, Shannon—don't come back.'

'That's the last thing I'd be likely to do,' she said bitterly, making her way to the door through a haze of tears. She stumbled along the hall to her own room, saw that it was blessedly empty, and clumsily shoved a chair under the door handle before collapsing on the bed in a storm of silent weeping that seemed only to increase rather than salve her pain. It was a long time before she slept, and then it was a restless sleep, torn by dreams full of menace and disaster.

For all that, she awoke early, feeling misery like a leaden weight in her breast. She stayed in bed for a while, tossing and turning as she tried to sleep even for half an hour longer; however, the more she strove for oblivion, the wider awake she became, and eventually she got up. One look at herself in the mirror—tear-swollen eyes and pale cheeks—and she headed for the shower. The hot, steamy water refreshed her physically. But it did more than that. It made her start to think again.

As she brushed her hair dry in front of the mirror, she recalled what it was that had so infuriated Blaise the very first time he had laid eyes on her, sitting alone in the dark in her mother's living room: it had been her lack of spirit. Her surrender to boredom and confinement. The fact that she had given up.

Now, was she not in danger of doing just the same thing? Most certainly her ill-timed visit to his room last night had been a disaster. Even now her cheeks burned at the thought of it. But today was a new day. Blaise, like herself, would have had time to think. Perhaps in the cool grey light of morning he would begin to realise that there must have been some truth to her story—for why else would she have intruded herself upon him in the middle of the night?

She finished drying her hair and dressed in a pair of slim-legged jeans and a tailored white shirt, a silk scarf knotted around her neck; a cool, practical outfit as different from her lacy nightwear as anything could be, she thought with a certain satisfaction. She took a deep breath to give herself courage, then, before she could change her mind, she marched along the hallway to his room. The sharp rat-tat of her knuckles against the door sounded deceptively decisive; as she waited, she was aware that her mouth was dry and her heart was thumping in her rib cage. No answer. She knocked again. Another long silence. She licked her lips and pushed open the door, fully expecting to find Blaise still in bed.

The room was empty. More than empty—deserted. She looked around her in growing consternation. The bed was neatly made. Of the welter of papers and maps and reports, there was no sign. The closet door had been left open; there were no clothes hanging there as there had been yesterday. No typewriter on the desk. No suitcase standing in the corner. No Blaise. . . .

He had gone, taking everything with him. Gone, not intending to return. Her throat closed with panic and ridiculously she opened the bathroom door, finding only still-damp towels and the lingering, masculine odour of after-shave. So he had not left last night. This morning he had showered and shaved . . . maybe he hadn't left yet. Maybe he was downstairs having breakfast, waiting to see her. To at least say goodbye.

She raced down the hallway, taking the stairs two at a time and narrowly avoiding a collision with Stepton, who was on his way back to the kitchen. 'Have you seen Blaise?' she gasped.

'He left over an hour ago, miss.'

Briefly she closed her eyes, fighting for breath. 'Left? To go where?'

'I have no idea.'

'You're sure he's gone?'

There was something like compassion in the faded old eyes. 'Yes, miss. He took the Ferrari.'

Not caring that he could see her bitter disappointment, she leaned against the wall. 'Oh, damn,' she said hopelessly.

'Mr Charles is having his breakfast now. Perhaps he could help you.'

Her face lit up. 'Of course—why didn't I think of that? Thanks!'

She hurried across the plush wool carpeting into the dining room, its tall square-paned windows revealing an expanse of cloudy, wind-torn sky and tossing branches. 'Charles!' she exclaimed unceremoniously. 'Where has Blaise gone?'

Fastidiously he wiped his mouth with the edge of his serviette, unconsciously echoing Stepton's words. 'I have no idea.'

'But didn't he tell you?'

'My dear child, I didn't ask. The days have long gone since I tried to keep track of my elder son's comings and goings.'

Shannon sat down heavily in one of the mahogany chairs. 'I need him,' she said, only realising afterwards how ridiculous this must have sounded.

'That is most unfortunate,' Charles said drily, methodically buttering a piece of toast. 'I am afraid you will have to wait until he sees fit to grace us with his presence again.'

There was something about this pedantic little speech that brought her chin up with a snap. '*Why* didn't you ask him where he was going?'

'I considered it none of my business.'

For the second time in less than twelve hours Shannon lost her temper. 'It's been a very long time since you considered anything to do with Blaise to be your business, hasn't it?' she cried recklessly. 'Since his mother died, to be exact.'

Charles half rose in his chair, his blue eyes as frosty as only his elder son's could be. 'Be quiet,' he snapped. 'I don't have to listen to this——'

'Oh yes, you do,' she retorted, jumping to her feet and leaning across the table. 'From the time his mother was killed, you ignored Blaise. Worse than that—you acted as though you hated him. You still do hate him, don't you? You don't give a damn that he was injured in Newfoundland saving a man's life!' A flicker of Charles's eyelids showed that this was new information to him. 'You didn't even know that, did you? You didn't care enough to ask. Just as this morning you didn't care enough to ask where he was going.'

Looking as though he was being racked, Charles said stiffly, 'I do care.'

'I don't believe you,' she stormed. 'You show no interest in his welfare or his whereabouts or his career. You speak to him as though he was a total stranger.'

'That's true,' said Charles with a quiet dignity that halted her spate of words. 'He is a stranger to me, and I admit that's largely my own fault. But don't accuse me of not loving him, Shannon—because that's not true.'

She sat down again, her green eyes wary. 'You *do* love him?'

'Yes. But over the years I've lost the art of communicating that love, Shannon. Nor do I really believe that he wants it any more.'

She rested her hand on his sleeve, her expression desperately sincere. 'He does, Charles. But like you, he's been afraid to show it. Afraid that you'd reject him again.'

He winced. 'After Ghislaine died, a part of me died, too. At first I couldn't bear to have Blaise around, because he could only be a reminder of happier days. So I pushed him away. And over the months and years that became a habit. . . . How do you know he still cares for me?'

Shannon sensed that he was afraid to believe her, so she injected all the confidence she could in her voice. 'He told me so.'

Charles stared at her thoughtfully. 'He must feel very close to you to share something so intimate.'

It was her turn to wince. 'Maybe he did feel that way —but he doesn't any more.'

'And is that related in any way to why you want to see him?' Because it was useless to deny it, she nodded miserably. 'We all thought you and Rick were in the process of patching things up.'

'Rick meant you to think that—but I don't love him at all.'

'You love Blaise.'

Her eyes swimming in tears, she said a low voice, 'Yes.'

'Very well,' Charles said briskly. 'As soon as I get to work, I'll contact his head office to see if he's gone back to Newfoundland. And I can check the university in Quebec where he was centred when he was doing all that research. In the meantime, why don't you ask Louise a little later on? There was always some kind of rapport between her and Blaise and she might be able to give you some idea of where he's gone. If neither of us get anywhere, tonight we'll send out a radio message via the police to have him get in contact with us.'

She blinked, beginning to realise why Charles was so successful a businessman and politician. 'He'd be furious,' she said faintly.

'Nonsense—it's time we got some of this cleared up,' Charles replied robustly.

'I'm sorry I yelled at you earlier,' she said, twisting her serviette into an untidy ball. 'I—I guess I just lost my temper. Which is really no excuse.'

'I'm not sorry. You said a number of things that needed saying.' He patted her hand. 'Now have some breakfast before you do anything else, and then a little later go and see Louise. And don't worry—everything will be all right.'

As though on cue, Stepton appeared in the doorway with a bowl of fresh fruit: melon and bananas and early strawberries. Realising with surprise that she actually was hungry, Shannon helped herself, following it with pancakes and maple syrup and two cups of Stepton's delicious coffee. It was still only nine-thirty, and two and a half hours could be expected to elapse before Louise put in an appearance. Gazing out of the window at a day that seemed more like March than June, Shannon knew she could not wait until midday; some sixth sense was pulling at her, urging her to find out, if at all possible, where Blaise had gone. It was important —too important to wait until Louise had completed her leisurely toilette. Swiftly the girl left the room, running up the stairs and into the opposite wing of the house, where Charles, Louise, and Rick had their rooms.

The first door, ajar, led into what was obviously Charles's quarters: austere, restrained, yet in excellent taste. Shannon tapped on the next door and a fretful voice called, 'Come in.'

If the first room had borne the unmistakable stamp of Charles's personality, this one was unquestionably Louise's. The shell-coloured rug was so thick that Shannon's feet sank into it; the windows and four-poster bed were draped in quantities of pale apricot chiffon, as was Louise herself. She was resting against the pillows with a breakfast tray on her lap, her jet black hair in a thick plait over one shoulder, her face looking naked without make-up. When she saw it was Shannon, she said without noticeable enthusiasm, 'Oh, hello. You're up early.'

'Yes. Louise, do you——'

'Something's wrong,' the older woman interrupted sharply. 'What is it? Is Rick——'

Shannon held tightly to her temper, knowing she could not afford to lose it again. 'No, it's nothing to do with Rick. At least, not directly. It's Blaise—do you know where he is?'

The exquisitely plucked eyebrows rose. 'No—should I?'

'He's gone.'

'My dear child, he's probably just gone to the post office to send off some of that horrendous paper work he was doing. Now, if you'll——'

'He's taken everything with him,' Shannon interjected, knowing she was not being particularly coherent but unable to help it.

The faintest of furrows creased the pale forehead. 'Well, perhaps he had a conference to attend or a meeting to go to. He'll be back.'

'I don't think so, Louise.' Shannon padded across the carpet and sat on the foot of the bed, her face strained and unhappy. 'You see, we had a terrible fight last night and now he's gone and I don't know where he is.'

'A fight? What about?'

'Rick.'

'Ah yes—Rick,' said Louise, her expression very cool. 'I gather you and Rick are engaged once more.'

If she was to get any co-operation from Louise at all, Shannon knew she had to be diplomatic; swallowing several retorts that came to mind, she said, 'No, we're not, Louise. Nor will we be. You see,' recklessly she burned her bridges, 'I'm in love with Blaise.'

The opaque grey eyes snapped open. 'My dear! This is very sudden.'

'Not really. It's just that I didn't realise what was happening until it was too late—you see, Blaise also thinks I'm in love with Rick.'

Louise sat up straighter, and Shannon could almost read her mind: her beloved Rick was safe, leaving her free to appreciate the intricacies of a love triangle. 'Something must be done,' said Louise with decisiveness normally quite out of character. 'Blaise has gone, you say?'

'Yes—he could be anywhere,' Shannon said despairingly.

'No, no, let's think. Where would he go?' She buttered a croissant thoughtfully, then nodded to herself once or twice. 'Yes, that would be it.'

'You know where he'd be?'

Instead of answering, Louise said abruptly, 'Does Blaise love you?'

The question was so unexpected that Shannon flinched.

'I don't think so. The reason I need to see him is to try and straighten things out—he thinks I'm Rick's mistress.' Her shoulders slumped miserably.

'Ridiculous man! One look at you should tell him you're nothing of the sort. It sounds as though he's jealous. And if he's jealous, it follows he's in love.'

Shannon's jaw dropped inelegantly; Louise's statements did have a crazy kind of logic. 'If only you were right,' she sighed. 'But the way he behaved last night, I think he hates me.'

Louise was no longer listening. 'His fishing lodge,' she said calmly. 'That's where he'll be.'

'How do you know?' Shannon asked incredulously.

'Because that's where he goes when he's in any kind of trouble, or unhappy, or simply needing to get away from it all. It's his escape, his retreat. Get me a piece of paper from the bureau and I'll draw you a map. You follow the river, then at North Bay. . . .' She drew a surprisingly neat map, carefully explaining the route to Shannon. 'Kipewa is the last little village. The lodge is on the shores of Lake Kipewa about four miles from the village—anyone there will direct you. Altogether, I suppose, it's about two hundred and fifty miles from here. The best thing would be to wait until this afternoon— Charles will get home around four, and then Sam can take you. It's not a journey to tackle on your own.' She smiled at the girl, patting her on the shoulder, the grey eyes once again sleepy. 'He'll be there—I'm sure of it.'

Shannon forced a smile, her green eyes still full of anxiety. 'I hope so. Thank you, Louise—I appreciate your help.'

Louise nodded slowly. 'One word of advice—it isn't always possible to take Blaise at face value. Oh, outwardly he's rich, successful, handsome, intelligent. All of that and more. But underneath—well, you know a little of his background. Underneath I think he's very much afraid of putting his trust in another person, particularly one he might love. For that person might go away. Or might turn out to be false, as Charles for so long was. If he felt that you had rejected him in favour of Rick—yes, he would find that very difficult to handle. If you can understand that, Shannon, and if the two of you can work out your differences, why, you'd have a man in a million.' She must have seen the fleeting surprise that Shannon had been unable to disguise, for she added with gentle mockery, 'Just because I dote on my own son, don't think I'm blind to Blaise's virtues.'

'I never have thought that, Louise, and I know he appreciates what you've done for him over the years.'

'Good.' The older woman glanced over at the antique gold clock on the mantel and said dismissively, 'I must get up, I have a luncheon date. Don't lose the map.'

'No. And Louise—thanks again.'

Shannon let herself out of the room, clutching the precious piece of paper, and walked slowly back to her room. She sat down on the bed, unfolding the map and recalling Louise's instructions; it looked very straightforward. She had her driver's licence in her handbag, and a credit card in case she ran into any trouble. She could be there in four or five hours. Six at the most. Whereas if she waited for Sam she wouldn't even get away until late afternoon. On her own, she could almost be there by then.

She gave herself a mental shake, horrified by the direction her thoughts were taking. She couldn't simply help herself to one of the Stratherns' cars and take off into the wild blue yonder—or rather, she amended ruefully, looking out of the window, the wild grey yonder. For it was raining now, a steady driving rain that looked like it would continue for hours: another reason to be sensible and wait for Sam's return.

Restlessly she paced up and down the carpet. Good

sense dictated she wait. Yet every instinct told her to leave now. It was almost as though Blaise himself was calling her . . . but that was nonsense. The reason he had left in the first place was to get away from her.

Back and forth her thoughts ranged. Go. Stay. Go . . . until she found herself hunting for a rain slicker and a pair of rubber boots in the cupboard, and checking her handbag to make sure she had everything she needed. She dashed off a quick note of apology and explanation to Louise, which she propped on the hall table in the foyer. Then she was out of the front door and running through the rain, head bent, to the garage.

Two cars were there: Louise's custom-built Thunderbird and the small Chevrolet hatchback. Sam had once shown her where the keys were kept, and it was the work of only minutes to open the garage door, back the Chevrolet out, and close the door again. Taking a few minutes to familiarise herself with the controls, she flipped on the windshield wipers and eased the car into first gear . . . she was off.

CHAPTER TWELVE

WHENEVER Shannon looked back on the next few hours, they seemed like a long-drawn-out nightmare. The road was slick with rain and totally unfamiliar to her, full of curves as it wound along the river's edge. There was the constant search for signposts, and the checking and rechecking of the map. The wind gusted against the little car, driving the rain like bullets into the windshield, and as the day progressed, her eyes began to ache with strain. But worse than that, and more debilitating, was the mental strain, for after all, Louise might be quite wrong:

it was entirely possible that Shannon could arrive at the fishing lodge and find it deserted, and the long drive would have been for nothing. Or—maybe worse—Blaise would be there, but would not want to see her, having just driven for six hours himself to get away from her. The only other possibility, that he would be pleased to see her and receptive to explanations about her supposed engagement to Rick, began to seem more and more remote as the slow afternoon hours passed.

She was driving steadily northwards now, the cities and towns long since left behind. The occasional village, a cluster of clapboard houses with a general store, a post office, and a garage, was all that broke the monotony of miles of wilderness, a vast, undulating forest of spruce and fir, wet and wind-whipped. Finally, however, the bright green road sign that said 'Kipewa' came into view; according to Louise's map, she had only four miles further to go. She slowed down as she approached the main street with its single crossroads and its flashing yellow light. There was a neon-lit drugstore on one corner, and on impulse she braked and pulled in to the kerb; a chocolate bar would taste good, she knew. As she waited for a couple of cars to pass before she crossed the street, she idly glanced over the row of parked vehicles at the gas station on the opposite corner. Suddenly her eyes widened in shock; the chocolate bar was forgotten. Pulled in to the spot nearest to the road was a black and red tow truck with a vehicle chained to its hoist: a Ferrari, the same dark blue as the Stratherns'. The windshield was shattered, and it was as though a giant hand had squeezed the left fender and headlight and the door on the driver's side, crumpling the metal as if it were paper.

For perhaps ten seconds Shannon stood rooted to the spot, her mouth dry with fear. It couldn't be Blaise's car. It couldn't be. Yet to find that colour and model of car only a few miles from his lodge . . . she darted an automatic look to left and right before running across the road to the garage. There was only one attendant, an elderly man sitting in a tilted-back chair, his hobnailed boots resting on the counter, which was pitted and worn from previous such encounters, his black-stemmed pipe emitting clouds of noxious smoke. Without waiting for him to speak, Shannon burst out, 'That car—the wrecked sports car. Whose is it?'

'Well now, that only came in an hour or so ago.' Another puff of smoke as he looked her up and down with a countryman's thorough, yet in no way ill-mannered, stare.

'Yes—but who does it belong to?'

'Terry brought it in. Terry!'

In an agony of suspense Shannon clasped her handbag to her breast, her fingers making permanent marks in the leather, she afterwards discovered. A younger man shambled in, his overalls caked with grease, his teeth a startling white in an oil-streaked face which exhibited the same unhurried friendliness as his companion's. 'Help you, ma'am?'

'The Ferrari—please, who owns it?'

'He made a real mess of it, didn't he?' Terry said comfortably. 'Mind you, it wasn't his fault. Old Abe had been into the whisky and drove his truck right at him. Don't know why he'd decided to come back to town so soon—he only arrived this afternoon.'

In this maze of muddled syntax the last phrase made Shannon's heart sink. 'Is the owner's name Strathern?' she blurted.

'Yeah—how'd you know?' Terry asked. 'You a friend of his?'

'Yes.'

She must have gone pale, for Terry, moving surprisingly fast, shoved her down into the sole remaining chair, first carelessly sweeping a pile of papers on to the floor. 'You okay?'

'What happened to him—to Mr Strathern?'

'They took him and Abe in the same ambulance over to Hopetown Hospital. Abe had sobered up some by then and he was cussing a blue streak. Your friend was kind of groggy himself—there was a lot of blood, but I don't think it was anything serious. He was lucky, mind you. That's a hell of a poor road at the best of times and with all the rain today, it'd be slicker'n an oil spill.'

Shannon closed her eyes, knowing Terry meant to be kind, but finding his description far from reassuring. An image of Blaise covered in blood rose like a ghastly spectre in her mind and she fought it back. Instead she focussed on something that was puzzling her. 'You said Mr Strathern was driving back to town—surely that's not right?'

'Yeah, he was—you could tell by the tyre marks.'

She frowned, wondering why Blaise should have left the lodge almost immediately after arriving. 'Where's Hopetown?' she asked abruptly.

'Ten miles back. Take a left at Kidston and go about four miles. Can't miss it.'

She stood up, willing her knees to stop trembling. 'Thank you for your help.'

'You be okay, ma'am? I'd drive you myself, but I promised Pete I'd have his carburettor back together by eight o'clock.'

He would have driven her, she knew. She gave him a generous smile, her eyes warm with gratitude. 'Thanks, Terry—I'll be all right. Goodnight.'

Back into the rain. Ducking her head, she ran across the street to the Chevrolet. Her hands were shaking so badly she had trouble getting the key in the ignition, and she forced herself to sit still for a minute, breathing deeply in an effort to calm herself. She knew where Blaise was, and in fifteen minutes she would see him, she told herself firmly. Terry had said he was not seriously hurt . . . although he must have been cut to have been bleeding. She suppressed a whole series of nightmare images, and carefully turned the car around, heading back the way she had come.

It was rapidly growing darker, the sky a towering mass of grey and purple clouds. Although there was no other traffic on the road, she was scared of driving too fast in case she missed the turn-off to Hopetown. But Terry's directions had been perfectly accurate; six miles from Kipewa the green signpost appeared and she turned left. Not far now. However, it seemed the closer she got to her destination, the more apprehensive she became; her hands were gripping the steering wheel so tightly that her knuckles were white and her wrists taut, and Terry's casual description had begun to assume the proportion of a nightmare. A car accident had robbed Blaise of her mother; another one had taken her own sight. What of this third one? What had it done to Blaise?

Through the gathering darkness she saw a cluster of yellow lights on the hill, where a carved wooden sign announced the Hopetown Hospital. Shannon turned up the paved driveway to the visitors' parking lot and drove into the nearest empty space. Putting the key in her handbag, she got out of the car and walked steadily across the pavement to the main entrance, her legs stiff as a wooden doll's. Pulling open the door, she felt warmth and the all-too-familiar hospital odour envelop her; her face very pale, she approached the desk. 'Do you have a Mr Blaise Strathern as a patient, please?' she asked the receptionist, a bored-looking girl with up-swept hair as bleached and brittle as straw.

'Strathern? I'll check.' The girl leafed through a card file. 'Emergency. Go to the end of the corridor, turn right, third door on the left.' Already dismissing Shannon, she began a minute inspection of her fingernails, which were painted the shade of overripe plums.

'Thank you,' Shannon said drily. She hurried down the corridor and turned as directed into a small reception area. A neat black and white sign said 'Please ring bell'. She did so, without result. Somewhere nearby a child was crying harshly and monotonously. In one of the chairs behind her an elderly man was sitting, staring down at the floor. No use to ask him.

She pressed the bell again and this time a nurse hurried in; beneath her professional manner Shannon could sense both tension and a controlled impatience. 'Can I help you?' the nurse asked politely.

'Is Blaise Strathern here?'

'Yes. He's nearly ready to leave. Have you come to get him?'

Shannon swallowed hard, her vision blurring momentarily. 'Can I see him?' she whispered.

A keen glance from the nurse. 'Of course. Come this way.'

Down another corridor with small treatment rooms on either side, in one of which was the child Shannon had heard crying; its sobs had subsided to a muffled hiccupping. The nurse pushed open the last door. 'Mr Strathern?' she said cheerfully. 'A visitor for you.' She ushered Shannon in, then bustled back the way she had come.

Not knowing what to expect, Shannon stopped in the doorway, her eyes very wide, her rain-damp hair a dark tangle around her face; she was still clutching her handbag to her breast.

The first thing that caught her eye was Blaise's shirt, flung across a chair; the bloodstains on it were a vivid scarlet, incongruous notes of colour in a room of greys and dull greens. As though pulled by a magnet, her eyes moved to the steel treatment table. Blaise was sitting on the edge of it, naked to the waist. The flesh across his ribs was grazed and raw; there was a purple bruise on his forehead and one cheek was disfigured by an ugly scrape. But his eyes, fastened on her, were the clear blue of a summer sky. He was alive, she thought confusedly, and sheer relief turned her knees to jelly; her head seemed to be floating, detached from her body.

'Shannon!' His voice had the deep timbre that was as familiar to her as her own voice. In one lithe movement he got down from the table.

Strong arms gripped her, pushing her down into a chair and lowering her head to her knees. Feeling sick and very cold, she breathed deeply for several minutes until gradually the world came back into focus. There was mud on the toes of her boots and the hem of her jeans were mud-splashed too. Blaise was so close to her that she could feel the warmth of his body and smell the sharp odour of the medication they had put on his torn skin.

'Better now?'

Slowly she raised her head, looking straight into the eyes so close to hers, and conscious of a strange feeling of breathlessness. 'Yes.' Unable to help herself, she touched his bare shoulder with her hand. 'I'm glad you're all right—I was so worried. He said there was a lot of blood, you see.'

'Who said?'

'Terry. At the gas station where they towed your car.'

'Oh, I understand. You saw the Ferrari——' He laughed without much amusement. 'Kind of a mess, isn't it?'

'That's why I was so scared.'

Blaise rested his own hand on top of hers, his smile very comforting. 'The blood was from nothing more complicated than a nosebleed. The only thing they were worried about here was the bang I got on the head—but they did a couple of X-rays, and there's no damage. My skull must be thicker than I thought. So I can leave any time. Are you sure you're all right?'

Not caring what she said, resting her cheek against their linked hands, she murmured, 'Now that I know you're safe, I'm fine.'

His free hand came up to stroke her hair. 'It goes curly in the rain, doesn't it?' he said inconsequentially. 'I presume you have a car here?'

'Yes—the Chevrolet.'

'Good. Let's go back to the lodge. We can talk there.' He straightened, pulling the girl to her feet. 'There's just one thing I want to say before we go. I've never been more glad to see anyone in my life than I was to see you come in that door.'

His words caught her unawares. A deep flush coloured her cheeks and she said uncertainly—and untruthfully, 'Oh—I see.'

'I don't think you do. There are a lot of things we need to talk about, Shannon—but not here.' He picked up the shirt with a look of distaste. 'I'll have to put this back on, I guess. And then let's get out of here.'

She could think of absolutely nothing to say. His simple words a few moments ago had filled her with wonder, yet she was almost afraid to believe in them. Fortunately, perhaps, an intern came in, and as he gave Blaise some last-minute instructions, her silence went unnoticed. Then they were going back down the corridor, past the receptionist—who was now reading a lurid-looking detective magazine—and out into the night. It was still raining. 'You wait here,' she said to Blaise. 'I'll bring the car over.'

'Nonsense,' he said firmly, tucking a hand under her elbow. 'I'm not an invalid—come along.' When he insisted on driving, she did not put up much resistance; all the wear and tear of the day seemed to have caught up with her, and she was bone tired. She leaned back in the seat and it seemed only seconds later that Blaise's voice announced, 'We're here. Wake up.'

'I wasn't asleep.'

'Then it was a very good imitation,' he grinned. 'Let's get inside—you can help me start the fire.'

As she hurried across the wet grass from the car to the house she had a confused impression of swaying fir trees and the rhythmic splash and lap of lakewater to her left; of a solid, graceful building constructed of stained cedar with a wide stone chimney and a stone-flagged verandah. Blaise unlocked the door, preceding her to flick on the lights. He turned up the thermostat, saying matter-of-factly, 'Electric heat—useful at times like this. The fire's laid in the fireplace. Touch a match to it, why don't you, while I change my shirt.'

Shannon had a couple of minutes to look around while the flames took hold of the kindling, crackling and spitting in the hearth. The interior was panelled in pine, with a lofty ceiling; handwoven curtains in muted shades of rust and orange were pulled across the windows while a thick shag rug in warm earth tones covered the floor. The furniture was an attractive blend of antique and modern, with books and pottery adding touches of colour. The whole effect was both casual and comfortable: a room to relax in.

Blaise had come back, buttoning an open-necked shirt over a pair of dark brown cords. 'Are you hungry?' he asked.

'Yes,' she said in surprise, 'I guess I am.'

'I brought some food with me—let's heat up some soup.'

Together they prepared and ate a simple meal, their conversation as though by mutual agreement on a light and conversational plane. But eventually they carried mugs of coffee into the living room where Shannon sank down on the carpet by the hearth, and more carefully Blaise followed suit. 'Your ribs must be sore,' she said, breaking the awkward little silence which had fallen since they left the kitchen.

'Yeah . . . but I'm lucky nothing's broken.'

'Yes, I suppose so.' She stared down at her mug, her hair falling like a curtain over her face.

'Look at me, Shannon.' Almost unwillingly she obeyed, her green eyes guarded and unsure. 'That's better.' He hesitated, then said slowly, 'When I had the accident I was headed back into town—I'd already been here and left.'

'I know. They told me that at the gas station.'

'Oh? Did you wonder where I was going?'

'I thought perhaps you'd forgotten something at the store.'

'No, Shannon. I was coming in to use the phone, because I wanted to speak to you.'

'Why?' she whispered.

He gazed at the flames, the light flickering over his scarred cheek. 'The farther away I got from Hardwoods, the more convinced I became that I'd been a fool to even listen to Rick, let alone to take his word for anything, as opposed to yours.' He rubbed his forehead. 'Something always happens to me in that house—there's too much of the past there. Too many memories of my mother. Too much of my father's rejection and of Rick's constant rivalry. . . .'

'Your father loves you, Blaise.'

'You'd have a job to convince me of that.'

'He told me so, this morning.'

She had his full attention now. 'What the hell are you talking about?'

So much had happened during the day that her confrontation with Charles seemed an aeon ago. 'When I came downstairs this morning, I was determined to talk to you,' she said, hurrying over that part so he wouldn't ask why. 'But no one knew where you'd gone—not Stepton, or your father.' She grimaced. 'I'm afraid I lost my temper with your father. I accused him of ignoring you, neglecting you, even hating you—oh dear, when I think of it now, I wonder how I could have said such awful things! Anyway, I did. His response was that he'd wanted to be close to you for a long time now, but he'd been afraid to make the first move—afraid you'd laugh at him, perhaps, or reject him as he'd so often rejected you. He really loves you, Blaise.'

His eyes bored into hers as though they would penetrate to her very soul. 'I have to believe you, don't I?' he said slowly. 'You wouldn't lie about something so important to me.'

'Of course not. It's true.'

'I wonder if after all these years, he and I can patch up our differences—I'd like to think we can.'

'I'm sure you'll be able to.' She spoke with complete confidence.

'If we do, it will be thanks to you, Shannon.'

She said uncomfortably, 'Nonsense—I didn't do anything.'

'Just why *did* you lose your temper?'

'I was upset,' she said shortly.

'Upset because I'd gone?'

Suddenly she knew she was finished with evasions and half truths. 'Yes.'

He nodded slowly, as though she had just confirmed something to him. 'Last night you told me you loved me. But I was so eaten up with jealousy and suspicion that I scarcely heard you. Did you mean it, Shannon?'

Her cheeks scarlet, not knowing where to look, she gasped, 'Yes.' Then, knowing she had to ask it, she said, 'You were *jealous*?'

'Of course I was. From the first moment I saw you, I

knew I wanted you for myself. But everywhere I turned, there was Rick. Your ex-fiancé, whom I thought you still loved. He'd informed me, you see, in quite specific detail, that you'd slept with him, and I had no reason to disbelieve him.'

'I told you I'd never made love with him!'

'Yes, you did. And I was beginning to believe you. But last night when I saw you in bed with him—I think I went a bit berserk, Shannon. I felt as though the bottom had dropped out of my world and all I wanted to do was to hurt you as I'd been hurt.' He reached over and took both her hands in his. 'That's not very admirable, is it? I'm sorry—more sorry than I can say. . . . Can you tell me what really happened?'

'He did it on purpose. I think he must have waited until he saw you return, and then he came to my room, knowing you'd have to see us when you walked past my door.' She shivered reminiscently. 'He told me that if he couldn't have me, he was going to make sure you didn't either.'

'That sounds like Rick,' Blaise said grimly. 'And I fell for it, didn't I?'

'I can hardly blame you,' she said, trying to be fair. 'It must have been a fairly convincing scene, after all.' They were still sitting with their hands linked, and from his flowed a current of warmth that seemed to reach every cell of her body. She felt as though she was on the brink of something momentous, to which all this talk of Charles and Rick was only a preview, necessary but essentially unimportant. As if he had read her mind, Blaise ordered, 'Tell me again that you love me.'

Shannon hesitated, for something was missing. Twice now she had said she loved him, but he had not responded in kind. Oh, he had said he wanted her; he had spoken of jealousy and hurt . . . but not of love. 'Why, Blaise?' she asked, her eyes mirroring her uncertainty.

'Because each time I hear you say it, I trust in it a little more.'

'Is it that hard to believe?'

There was pain in his face, and it roughened his voice when he spoke. 'For me, yes.'

Feeling her way, she said, 'Because the people who've loved you have left you or pushed you away. Is that it?'

'That's it, Shannon,' he agreed heavily. 'I couldn't bear it if you did that.' Although she ached to reassure him, some instinct told Shannon to remain silent. He was playing with her fingers now, his eyes intent on what he was doing. 'I have never in my life told a woman I loved her. I was starting to wonder if I ever would—I thought there must be some basic lack in me, some abnormality. Until I met you.' He looked up, his expression strained and intense. 'You changed everything. I'd read about love at first sight and always dismissed it as romantic fiction until it happened to me. I walked into your mother's house and there you were, and I knew that the search I hadn't even been aware of was over: I'd found the woman I wanted to spend the rest of my life with.'

Shannon said faintly, 'I thought you despised me that first evening.'

'Far from it, my dear. But it wasn't the time for the truth. I didn't want you to come to me out of need or dependence because of your blindness. I wanted you to come as an independent woman—out of joy and love, not out of fear.'

'So you gave me back my sight.' Tears misted the eyes that not long ago had been unable to see him.

'And—or so I thought—inadvertently caused you to become involved with Rick again.'

'Not really. You see, I kept comparing him with you— to his detriment.'

His hands tightened around hers. 'I believe that now. Do you remember at the hospital I told you how glad I was to see you? You proved something to me today, Shannon, by following me for miles through the wind and the rain because it was important that you see me.' With a humility that made her want to weep, he added, 'I'm not used to having anyone care that much—do you understand what I'm trying to say?'

'Yes, I understand,' she replied huskily. 'I'd follow you to the ends of the earth, Blaise.'

'And I you.' His hands moved to her elbows and he pulled her to her feet. 'Because I love you with all my heart, dearest Shannon, and I always will.'

She had thought she had known happiness before, but it had only been a pale imitation of the golden tide of joy that carried her into his arms. His mouth was gentle yet sure, his kiss reiterating the commitment he had made in words. Ever afterwards the tang of woodsmoke and the patter of rain on the roof would recall that perfect moment for Shannon . . . when she knew she was loved as she herself loved. With complete trust she gave herself up to his embrace, her eyes closed, her body flooded with a sweetness that, as his hold tightened, began to pulse with desire. His kiss became the whole world to her. He pressed his mouth to hers, his hand delicately stroking the full curve of her breast until it swelled to his touch. Somehow her blouse was pushed from her shoulders and his face was buried in the sweet-scented valley of her flesh; she held him to her, her cheek against his hair, her lips murmuring his name, knowing there was nothing of herself she could withhold from him.

From a long way away she heard him breathe against her skin, 'I want you, Shannon. Oh God, how I want you!'

Very quietly she said, 'And you may have me, body and soul. Now—and for ever.'

Blaise went very still. Then he raised his head, his vivid eyes desperately serious. 'You've never made love with a man before, have you, Shannon?'

'No—never,' she replied, searching his face, afraid that she had said the wrong thing a moment ago.

'Yet you would give yourself to me now, wouldn't you?'

No matter what the consequences, she had to be truthful. 'Yes, I would, Blaise.'

The light in his eyes shone straight into her heart. 'A while ago I spoke of proof—how you'd proved you loved me by following me here. And now you offer me another proof—the gift of your body.'

'I love you, Blaise.' It seemed the only reply she could make.

'I know you do, Shannon. I know you do . . . and God knows I want to make love to you.' His hands slid from her breasts to the slenderness of her waist, so that she quivered with delight. 'Will you think me very old-fashioned if I say I'd rather wait—we can be married in three days' time.'

Sheer wonderment blazed in her jade green eyes. 'You want to marry me?'

'Well, of course,' he said in surprise. 'I won't rest until I've got that gold band on your finger. And then——' His grin was so boyish that her happiness overflowed into laughter. '—and then you'd better watch out, Mrs Strathern. Because it will be you who won't be getting much rest.'

Of their own accord her fingers caressed the hard planes of his chest and the strong, muscular column of his throat, pulling his head down to hers. 'Nor will you, I promise.'

He gathered her closer, wincing from the pain of his ribs. 'Here I finally have you to myself, and I can't even hug you,' he complained jokingly. Then, more seriously, 'You haven't said you'll marry me yet, Shannon—will you?'

'Yes, Blaise.' Her eyes travelled over his face, memorising each beloved feature. 'I'm so glad I can see you,' she murmured. 'But even if I were still blind, I would never doubt that you loved me. It's as though . . .' she paused, searching for the right words. 'It's as though my heart can see into yours and read what's written there.'

'We were both blind for a while, Shannon. You, physically. I, because of jealousy and fear. But not any longer.'

'No,' she said, her eyes shining into his with the joyous vision of a future shared together. 'We can both see the truth now—the truth of a love that will last for ever.'

Harlequin Plus
A WORD ABOUT THE AUTHOR

A search for part-time work that could be done at home led Sandra Field to her career as a Harlequin author. Her first manuscript, which took a year to complete, was *To Trust My Love* (Romance #1870). Published in 1975, it was set in Canada's Maritimes, the richly historic and dramatically scenic provinces of eastern Canada that Sandra calls home.

She has the distinction of being Harlequin's first North American author. And whether writing about *The Storms of Spring* or *The Winds of Winter*, she tends to set her love stories in the Maritime Provinces so dear to her.

Sandra Field holds a degree in science from Dalhousie University in Halifax, Nova Scotia, and before becoming a full-time author she worked as a laboratory technician. Apart from being an avid reader of Harlequins and other fiction, her interests include cross-country skiing, snow-shoeing, gardening, bird-watching and listening to classical music (Brahms is her favorite composer).

Sandra Field's fans may be interested to know that she occasionally collaborates on a book with her best friend. When she does, the author's name appears as Jan MacLean. To date, four Romances have been published under this pseudonym.

FREE!

A hardcover Romance Treasury volume
containing 3 treasured works of romance
by 3 outstanding Harlequin authors...

...as your introduction to Harlequin's
Romance Treasury subscription plan!

...almost 600 pages of exciting romance reading
every month at the low cost of $6.97 a volume!

A wonderful way to collect many of Harlequin's most beautiful love
stories, all originally published in the late '60s and early '70s.
Each value-packed volume, bound in a distinctive gold-embossed
leatherette case and wrapped in a colorfully illustrated dust jacket,
contains...
• 3 full-length novels by 3 world-famous authors of romance fiction
• a unique illustration for every novel
• the elegant touch of a delicate bound-in ribbon bookmark...
  and much, much more!

Romance Treasury

...for a library of romance you'll treasure forever!

Complete and mail today the FREE gift certificate and subscription
reservation on the following page.

Romance Treasury

An exciting opportunity to collect treasured works of romance! Almost 600 pages of exciting romance reading in each beautifully bound hardcover volume!

You may cancel your subscription whenever you wish! You don't have to buy any minimum number of volumes. Whenever you decide to stop your subscription just drop us a line and we'll cancel all further shipments.